how loveta got her baby

how loveta got her baby

STORIES

NICHOLAS RUDDOCK

*To Heike,
with friendship,
Nicholas Ruddock
March 13/2014*

BREAKWATER

P.O. BOX 2188, ST. JOHN'S, NL, CANADA, A1C 6E6
WWW.BREAKWATERBOOKS.COM

COPYRIGHT © 2014 Nicholas Ruddock
LIBRARY AND ARCHIVES CANADA CATALOGUING IN PUBLICATION
Ruddock, Nicholas, author
How loveta got her baby / Nicholas Ruddock.
Short stories.
ISBN 978-1-55081-475-0 (pbk.)
I. Title.
PS8635.U34H69 2014   C813'.6   C2014-900560-1

ALL RIGHTS RESERVED.
No part of this publication may be reproduced, stored in a retrieval system or transmitted, in any form or by any means, without the prior written consent of the publisher or a licence from The Canadian Copyright Licensing Agency (Access Copyright). For an Access Copyright licence, visit www.accesscopyright.ca or call toll free to 1-800-893-5777.

We acknowledge the support of the Canada Council for the Arts which last year invested $24.3 million in writing and publishing throughout Canada. We acknowledge the Government of Canada through the Canada Book Fund and the Government of Newfoundland and Labrador through the Department of Tourism, Culture and Recreation for our publishing activities.

PRINTED AND BOUND IN CANADA.

Breakwater Books is committed to choosing papers and materials for our books that help to protect our environment. To this end, this book is printed on a recycled paper that is certified by the Forest Stewardship Council®.

to
Cheryl,
to the Keepings
and the Mays

con-tents

how loveta got her baby... 9
squid... 19
mistaken point... 21
shuffle... 39
how eunice got her baby... 41
strait... 51
scenario 2 a.m.... 53
fog... 63
telescope... 73
the housepainters... 75
otto bond... 91
sculpin... 105
rickshaw... 107

the alchemists... 117
how it was for them... 119
summer... 129
pivot... 131
how kiziah got her baby... 133
the steamer... 151
clothespin... 165
the eye... 167
burin... 179
rigor mortis... 181
the earlier misfortunes
    of justin peach... 197
breathing like that... 207

how loveta got her baby

LOVETA ROSE GRANDY was a pretty girl. She had blonde hair that she worked up in tight curls but she didn't fuss like the others. She didn't have to. Back then she had a boyfriend whose name was Philip John Savoury, and he worked at a decent kind of job. He was an apprentice welder near the airport. Weekdays, he studied welding from nine to five, and on weekends he picked up Loveta in a car he had, and they drove somewhere, and then they went for a walk.

"What kind of car is this?" she said to him the very first time.

"What kind of car?"

He had to look over at the dashboard before he said, "Camaro."

It was a borrowed car from some other welder who worked nights and slept days. It had bucket seats.

Where'd they go? Well, the first place they went, the very first time, was Signal Hill. Everybody went up there and everybody went up to the top and pulled over and looked at the view. As for Loveta Rose Grandy and Philip John Savoury, they only drove to the bottom of the hill and then they pulled over in the Camaro. The road was so steep there, they had to turn the wheels to the curb. Then they got out and walked through the Battery. There was a big house there half-hidden by trees, with old-fashioned fencing, sticks interwoven together, but there were holes in that fence that let chickens through, out onto the road. But there was next to no traffic, because the road was narrowing down to about ten feet, so the chickens were okay.

"Hey look, there's a brown chicken," she said.

"It's red," he said.

"Russet," she said.

They argued over the colour of the chicken but they didn't feel angry at all, it was just another way of laughing together. I mean, what's a chicken doing here, they both thought. It was a brown-red chicken, some kind of mixture, and it had a kind of nasty look in its eye while it picked up pebbles and walked around like a boss or a foreman.

"There's lots like that at work," said Philip John.

"Teachers too," said Loveta.

She was still at Holy Heart of Mary. She had those skirts from there, the ones with the pleats, but today she had on blue jeans.

"Wear jeans," her mother had said to her before she left, "wear jeans in the car."

Then she watched her baby girl as she went off in the Camaro with the young welder boy and then Loveta's mother imagined Loveta in the front seat with her knees up a bit, and she pictured her first in a skirt, and then in jeans.

That's why the jeans, she said to herself.

Meta Maud, she didn't worry much about Meta Maud, she more or less had her head together.

By then the Camaro was gone off down Pennywell Road.

After Loveta and Philip John Savoury left the chicken behind, they walked out along the road which went up and down beside the harbour. There was a lot of noise from winches and motors and there were seagulls standing on the roofs of the little houses they passed. There was a blustery wind which was cool and the seagulls all faced in the same direction, out the Narrows.

"There's a seagull, Philip John," she said.

"That's a herring gull," he said.

"It's a tern," she said.

"It's a diving duck," he said.

But they both knew it was no diving duck. How could a diving duck stand on a roof?

"Look at the mess they make," said Loveta.

There were a lot of white spots on the tarred-up roofs.

"Guano," said Philip John.

"Wouldn't want that on me," she said.

"Loveta," said Philip John, "that's nature's way, it's a free patch job for the people of the Battery. Once there was a fisherman here with a bad roof one winter and the gulls came by, fixed up the roof free of charge. One day water poured down the stovepipe and it sizzled on the stove, and the next day, after the gulls, it was dry as dry can be."

"I don't believe that," she said.

"It's the miracle of nature's fluids, Loveta, one of them anyway," he said.

He took her arm then to help her step onto the grass that grew up near Chain Rock. Now they could feel the wind getting stronger, thumping against them in spasms, and there was an old bunker there from the war. They walked in front of that and stood on the edge of the cliff. There were no more houses now, they'd gone past them all and the noises from the winches and the motors were gone and they could feel the power of the waves as they hit on the rocks below. He let go of her arm. He wasn't all

HOW LOVETA GOT HER BABY

over her all the time, he gave her space.

"Look, blueberries," he said.

"Past ripe," she said.

"Oh no, these are fine."

He bent down and picked a few that looked pretty good.

"They were better two weeks ago," she said.

"Oh, the first bit of frost just peps 'em up, open your mouth," he said.

Philip John Savoury put a blueberry on the tip of Loveta Grandy's tongue and she chewed it and swallowed it.

Her tongue was pink.

"That's good," she said, "I admit that's good."

Then the sun came out and it was so warm they kept on walking. The path got rougher and there was one point where they had to hang onto a chain that was drilled into the rockface. The path was only a foot wide. Loveta knew she'd die if she let go.

"You go first," said Philip John, "You fall, I'll throw myself over, catch you on the way down."

"Like Tinkerbell," said Loveta.

"That's right," said Philip John.

He watched her cross the slippery rock where only a goat should go, the nice blue jeans she had and the sweater with deer on it. Then he crossed over too and there was room to breathe, the path widened and went up and up in stages. There were wooden steps here and there that made it easier.

I wonder what she's up to now, Loveta's mother said to herself, I wonder.

She saw the Camaro pulled over somewhere by a beach, the one at Middle Cove. She saw the welder boy lean over the gearshift and turn his head to the right and she saw Loveta hunker down a bit and close her eyes. Then Loveta's mother turned her mind from that possibility and, instead, she saw them walk along the beach, not even touching. Then they jumped out of the way of a big wave that surprised them both with the strength it had. Loveta got a soaker, it went right through her jeans past her waist. That was a close call. The welder came over and acted real protective, he wrapped his arms around Loveta but what did he really want? A dog ran by after a stick and there was a picnic and there were lots of people there at Middle Cove.

At Signal Hill, they'd gone a long way now, all the way up by North Head and they'd turned the corner from town so all you could see was the bare rock, the ocean hundreds of feet below, and the sky. The wind was cooler again. He put his arm around her shoulder.

"I like the moose and the snowflakes knitted on your sweater," he said.

"They're reindeer," she said.

His arm was still there but he hadn't pulled her in tight. She leaned towards him.

"Look," she said, "the snow falls on the reindeer, it falls heavy on their backs, but it doesn't pile up."

"The heat of their bodies, I bet, melts it," he said.

A jogger came by out of nowhere with a Walkman on and ran past them. Philip John took his arm off her. Now they could see the waves off Cape Spear and the waves off Fort Amherst.

"Let's go off the path a bit," he said.

"Let's," she said.

Loveta's mother finished with the laundry. What about those jeans, she thought, what about those jeans? Maybe that wasn't such a good idea, after all. Say Loveta got a soaker right through, from the wave at Middle Cove. Say she got a chill with those blue jeans soaked right through and then she gets back in the car with the welder boy. Those jeans'll never dry like that, he might say, never ever. Take those jeans off, Loveta. You'll catch your death of cold. He looked like he could say that with a twinkle in his eye. He was that type. Loveta's mother knew right off the first time she saw him, when he got out of that Camaro and walked up to the door. She saw Loveta lift her hips up in the front seat and she saw her wiggle out of the jeans. She peeled them right off, down past her ankles. Put them up there on the heater vents, the boy said, and he started up the car, and all the steam rose out of the jeans and misted up like a fog and covered up the windows on the inside. You couldn't see in and you couldn't see out.

The footing there on the brow of North Head was good. It was scrabbly stone with grit in it, you couldn't slip if you tried.

"Sandstone," said Philip John.

"Shale and granite and soapstone," said Loveta.

"Let's sit down there," he said.

He pointed to where there was a boulder and some grass and some sun and the waves from the open sea clamoured in through a crevice in the rock, below.

Inside the Camaro, Loveta's mother saw the mist on the windows. Those little panties you got on, they're wet too, he said. Loveta lifted up her hips again, and my God she wasn't even shy when she hooked off the panties and then she was bare naked from the waist down. Hang them on the mirror he said, up there. They'll dry in no time, they're so tiny, so flimsy. Like nothing at all. Now a simple skirt could have dried off by itself, or Loveta could have held it up out of the water when the wave came. Loveta's mother blamed herself now, she blamed herself for what she saw. The boy said, put your right knee out that way, to the door, you'll feel the blow from the heater better with your leg like that. Then Loveta's mother said Jeez to herself and lit up a smoke. She didn't want to watch anymore.

Loveta Grandy and Philip John Savoury climbed down the slope to the big boulder. It was as big as the Camaro, and there was sunshine on the lee side, out of the wind. They sat down on the grass and leaned up against the rock, shoulder to shoulder.

"I've never been out this far before," she said.

There was nothing on the ocean but birds and more birds and behind them there was nothing but the rock. They looked at each other.

Maybe she didn't want to watch anymore but Loveta's mother couldn't help herself. Loveta was her baby, the last daughter she had. Loveta's mother heard a little click as the welder boy reached under the front seat and released the lever there. Then he pushed back with his feet and the driver's seat slid back so there was more room for him to turn and move around. He reached over and put his hand on Loveta, high up on her leg, up high on the inside of her thigh where the skin is thin and real sensitive. He laid it there casually and Loveta didn't twitch, she didn't move away. In fact she did the opposite. Rain spattered now on the outside of the window. The shadows of the Middle Cove picnic people ran by their car. There's no one can see us now, said the boy. Then he limbered up and shifted out of his seat and tried to get over top of Loveta. Thank God he still had his clothes on. Damn these seats, the boy said, damn these bucket seats. He gave up and sat back down on his own side and he said, Loveta, try this, get up on top. She was so small, it was no problem for her. Especially with the clothes she'd taken off. She was up and over top of the gearshift like she was a pine marten. Then she settled herself down on his lap, the steering wheel in tight behind her. Brazen, Loveta. Now he had his hands on her back.

Loveta's mother went to the front door and looked out. Maybe the Camaro would show up, all of this would stop.

Philip John Savoury felt the grit from the sandstone bite into his shoulders when he turned to look at Loveta Rose Grandy. He loved the way her curls fell. He turned his face a bit towards her and she did the same. They kissed. The first touch of their lips was cold from the wind and they didn't move, they just kept their lips like that and then they backed off.

"We're all alone with the sky," he said.

"There's ground," she said.

They kissed again. Their lips hadn't moved far apart, so it was easy.

"Actually there's rocks too," he said.

"It's wet, winter's coming on," she said.

They stood up. He brushed the dirt off the back of her jeans.

"You're damp there," he said.

She looked at her watch.

"It's time to walk back."

"Okay."

She took his arm for the climb back up to the path.

The worst fears are the ones you don't know, thought Loveta's mother. She saw the welder boy pull open his jeans under Loveta. He had the button kind. Loveta ground herself down on him hard, like she was careless. You couldn't hear the waves anymore from the Cove, there was a hum in the car. All of a sudden the welder boy said get off, Loveta, get off get off! And she tried to pull herself back up and away but the steering wheel jammed in there fast on her back. She felt what happened, what he did. It was too late for her. What a mess it made when she did get off, when she lifted herself up and the welder boy held his head in his hands. There you go, Loveta, he said, look what you done, look what you done, oh damn these bucket seats.

"I enjoyed the walk," said Loveta, when they got back down to the Battery and they stood beside the Camaro. He opened the door for her. It was warm inside. They drove back onto Duckworth Street and up Military Road and soon they were stopped outside Loveta's house.

The livingroom curtains moved.

"There's your mother," he said.

"That's her, she worries way too much," said Loveta.

"Say hello to her."

She got out. She blew him a little kiss from the window, so her mother couldn't see.

"Where to next week, Philip John?" she asked.

She leaned back into the car.

"Pouch Cove, the Cape?" he said.

"I don't want to go that far," she said.

"Middle Cove then, we can watch the waves."

"Good, I'd like that. Dress warm. Bye."

She pulled herself back from the car window and the Camaro drove off.

Look at her, said Loveta's mother, look at her, like there's nothing wrong at all.

squid

THOMAS KEEPING, 12, of Belleoram, knew he was being foolish when, at school, he publicly proclaimed the founding of the "Giant Squid Club," of which he would be Founding President and Chief Scientific Officer, and he felt doubly foolish when the only other student to sign up was Cyril Savoury, then in his second year in grade two, unable to concentrate at all and with a lazy eye that wandered into orbits never seen before by any of the ophthalmologists in St. John's, a boy who could nevertheless sign his own name over and over and over again in a cursive script of mediaeval precision; Thomas Keeping declared that Cyril Savoury was Goodwill Ambassador for the Giant Squid Club, and every Friday and Saturday night throughout the spring the two lone members would pitch their canvas tent down by the barasway, under the shadow of the rockface Iron Skull, and build a small fire, and wait for the blowing of the whales and the slap of their bodies as they rose, exhausted, nearly drowned, and Cyril and Thomas could see, even at midnight, the scars left by tentacles suction-cupped into blackened flesh, and they could see deep cuts from the beak of the giant squid oozing whale blood into the slithered brine, but that was as close as the Founding President and the Goodwill Ambassador ever came to the giant squid, this circumstantial evidence of submarine battles, of tentacled arms clamped over the jaws of the leviathan, force pulling them both down into depths where the pressure said: let go.

mistaken point

HENRY FIANDER HAD nothing to do with the initial conception of the plan. Sure, he was there in town by birth, and he was there by personal association, but it was still only by the purest chance that he was the one who got lucky. If it hadn't been for that, for that strike of good fortune, then the girl he loved, Eunice Cluett, could have taken off with someone else forever. She could have taken that positive life force everybody knew she had, she could have taken her warmth, her courage, and even those normal sexual desires of hers which at that time were lying dormant, unanswered by an outside agency, and she could have used them all up, consumed them, burned them up like a bonfire with a stranger somewhere else. That could have happened but it didn't, and why? Because Aaron Stoodley was a friend of Henry's, and Aaron Stoodley always had an eye out for better times, and one night, when Aaron was walking through his grandmother's livingroom and she was watching TV, he stopped beside her and looked. It was as simple as that. It was like someone picked up a clock, wound it, and it started to tick. Or like someone rubbed the magic lamp and out came a genie with a smile on his face.

There, on the television, were pictures they were showing from the war in Iraq. People ran around in banged-up streets. They had statues and tablets and huge bowls and god-knows-what in their arms. They held other things that were hard to make out, the way the film jumped up and down, and often they didn't run, they just walked and smiled at the cameraman and held up whatever they had like it was a prize.

"What's all that?" Aaron said to his grandmother.

There were broken buildings in the background, rubbled, destroyed. There were stone columns bent at angles. There were chips of rock and marble and dust and people running here and there and they all wore the same baggy white clothes. There was so much fine dust in the air, it was like they were rushing in and out of fog.

"It's Arabs," said his grandmother, "Arabs getting by. They're after running off with the old things. Antiques, treasures of all kinds."

"They stealing it?"

"Stealing? I don't know I'd call it that, they're just getting by the best they can. Look at their teeth, mind you, those Arabs, Aaron, they got the whitest teeth I ever seen, every one."

His grandmother, who raised him, sat and smoked menthol cigarettes most of the day. She made rugs, mittens, scarfs. She had a pile of wool at her feet and she favoured the colour yellow even though there were some who said, "Priscilla, you make those out of blue, they'd sell faster. Put some blue trim on, anyway." But she had her own mind and there was a store on Water Street where they stocked all the stuff she made, yellow mittens, yellow sweaters, yellow gloves. If you bent down and buried your nose in those mittens and sweaters, according to Aaron Stoodley, you could smell menthol cigarettes, faint but pure. For him, it was like being transported home again. Those times he worked in town, which were several, down he'd go down to that store just for the olfactory pleasure. He'd bury his head there in the yellow wool till the store personnel came by and they said, "Okay, Aaron Stoodley, that's enough of that, enough of that olfactory pleasure of yours, you get out of here now."

Aaron loved his grandmother. When she said, "No, those Arabs, I don't think I'd call that stealing," she didn't know it but Aaron had the moral go-ahead for the plan that percolated through his head.

He sat down and watched the rest of the program and then he put on his coat and walked down to the Legion. He knew Henry Fiander would be there.

"Rack 'em up," he said as he walked to the pool table. "We are about to become liberators of stone. Baghdadians."

That was the way Aaron Stoodley talked. He dressed everything up, made it sound finer than it was and Henry never knew, right off, which way to look at what he said.

Midafternoon, the two of them had the whole place to themselves. There was a weak light that came through the front window, on the ocean side, and there was a hanging light over the pool table that cast a blue-green cone of chalk dust, floating in the air, a bit like that dust that rolled by the cameras in Baghdad.

Aaron chalked up his cue right then and delivered a mighty blow to the white ball and there was a wild scattering all over the table. It made a clash, an echoing noise bigger than a bowling alley. Then all was still again.

"It's like a sepulchre in here," said Aaron, "like something dead. Your turn."

Henry looked at the table. Despite the smash that Aaron Stoodley had delivered, the cue ball had slid down into an impossible spot in one corner and there was nothing easy to do. It was blocked in by a jumble of four reds, all of them leaning on each other. It was hopeless.

"This is a symbol of my life," said Henry.

He hit the cue ball and there was more noise and more running around of all the colours on the table. One of the red balls teetered on the edge of a pocket and then, even though the force of gravity said it should fall, it didn't.

"Don't get down on yourself, Henry," said Aaron, "that's the worst. Somedays we're not so bad off here, other days I don't know."

Then he told Henry what he'd seen on TV.

"Baghdad, the whole place over there's a mess. It's shambled, it's wrecked, there's nothing there to lose. That remind you of anything, Henry?"

"No not really."

"It's like us, here with the fish, like right here, that's what it reminds me of. But the difference is this: over there, once they get their hands on those antique treasures, off they go to Paris France, to the black market. They get hundreds of thousands of dollars then for one piece of stone with writing on it. Scratches really. Here, on the other hand, we get a boatload of fish, illegal too mind you, and we get nothing. Nothing. Zero. And that's the whole idea, Henry. Remember those fossils out there, Mistaken Point?"

So were mentioned the fateful words for the first time. Mistaken Point.

Sure, Henry Fiander remembered. They'd been out there all their lives. Five miles or more out of town, right down by the edge of the sea on a black tilted floor of rock, all kinds of nice patterns. They looked like fishbones, or plants, you could walk on them, slide around on a nice day, pack a lunch, enjoy the breeze. What's that? they'd say. Looks like a leaf, a giant bug, a fish with legs. You name it, those fossils could look like anything. All of them were out there on a shelf of black rock the size of, well, say the Legion dance floor stretched out sideways. A dance floor balanced out over the ocean. You slid down from the edge of the meadowgrass, there you were.

"Henry, all those rocks, those fossils, they're priceless. Same as the stones in Baghdad."

"Priceless?"

"That's the word those professors used when they came out here. You remember?"

"Sort of. In their pick-ups, their Zodiacs, their floppy hats, yes I remember."

"Right," said Aaron, "they all had the same beard, we laughed at that, they had their fancy, heavy-duty klieg lights set up on tripods in the middle of the day."

"They took a million photographs. They had wetsuits."

"More to the point, Henry, they said that these scratchings are priceless national treasures, a million years old, a trillion years old or whatever. Priceless, that was the word. And what else, Henry? They said, you here are the local guardians for these treasures."

Aaron had already put his cue down against the table. It looked like he'd finished playing pool.

"Local guardians. So the way I see it now is this. There are hundreds of thousands of American dollars waiting for us, we are the local guardians, right now on our own doorstep, buddy."

The two of them went outside. There was a chill to the wind that whipped at them both and they looked out to the ocean, which was flat and grey with just a ripple on it. They wrapped scarves around their faces, over their noses.

"Now we look like Arabs, sort of, scarves like this," said Aaron Stoodley.

His voice came muffled through the cloth.

"Hard to breathe into this wind," said Henry.

So they took off their temporary facial-protection disguises, went inside, locked up, went home and the next morning the two of them drove out there, to the Point, or at least as close as they could get, before the road ran out.

"Time to reconnoitre," Aaron said, "make sure the fossils are there, still ripe for the picking."

"Where could they go after all those millions of years?"

"You never know with nature. There could be a cataclysm. They could rise and fall into the deep. Witness Mount Vesuvius, Krakatoa East of Java, and the various implosions within our lifetime. Henry, you can never be too sure."

It was a long walk from where the road ended to the fossil bed and the whole countryside had a wild feeling about it. There was miles of sky. The two of them were a good half hour up and half hour down in the bog and the crowberry. There were no trees because the wind, over the years, blew anything higher than a rabbit right over, or bent it down so far that it reattached itself to the earth and lay there, servile.

Finally there they were. They stood at the edge of the meadow where it tipped down to the sea. It was almost calm out on the ocean, very little surge coming in and the black shale, where the fossils rested, was dry. Footing was good. There was a bit of raggedness on the horizon, that's all.

"Oh they're perfect," said Aaron. "Look at them. There's our little gold mine. All accounted for."

The fossils were impressive, there was no denying it. You couldn't put your foot over them, they were so big, and there were hundreds of them plain as day, like patterns on a black shiny quilt.

"They do seem to be stuck in there," said Henry.

"That's right," said Aaron. "We need technical help to jar these guys loose. But we got the inventory, that's for sure."

They headed on back and thought about what was next.

"You know, what we need, we need Black and Decker,

something like that, we just can't just peel them off like labels," said Aaron.

The more they thought about it, the more they needed another hand. An accomplice with tools. The money was going to be good enough, a three-way split would be fine.

"Eunice?" Henry Fiander said, as though he just thought of it.

When Henry looked back upon the adventure much later, this was the one thing he did. He was the one who suggested Eunice. The rest of it all just cooked along without much more input from him.

"Eunice Cluett? She'd fit," said Aaron. "Her father had tools in his day, lots of them. I don't know what she thinks of us though. Familiarity breeds contempt, the way she looks at us, I don't know, Henry."

They'd all gone through school together.

"Maybe we do not fit high in her esteem, is what I mean."

"I think she'd let bygones be bygones, if there are any," said Henry.

"She could use the money, that's for sure," said Aaron Stoodley.

Eunice Cluett had blonde hair. Henry could see it when he thought of her, how she kept it up in a ponytail. At the present time, there she was with her two-year-old in a small house down by the shore. There was no man around that anyone could see, and her clothesline was right now double-bow-stringed down with the weight of rabbits she caught herself.

A long long time ago, when the fossils were a few years younger, Henry Fiander lost the grade seven spelling bee to Eunice Cluett. The word she got, the one he missed? He remembered it still: *tarmac*.

"How can you lose with that?" Henry's father said back then.

"By not spelling it right," said his mother. "That Eunice Cluett, she's as smart as she is pretty."

Being smart didn't save Eunice from some kind of trouble though. Her family moved away, closed down the house, shuttered it blind, and then all of a sudden she was back, all alone, and now she had a baby girl, Queenie, along for the ride.

"Don't ask her where Queenie came from," everybody said. "It'll all come out in the wash, give her time."

Aaron and Henry walked over to her place.

"Well hi there, boys," she said through the screen door.

"Eunice, how'd you like eight dollars for all them rabbits?" said Aaron.

"Eight dollars? I don't think so. They're worth more than that. And they sure look better than you do, Aaron Stoodley, they got less facial hair."

Her screen door had a tear in it at dog level. Aaron picked up on that right away.

"Miss Cluett," he said, "granted my appearance is somewhat grizzled, but let me ask you this—how'd you like to fix up this here fractured screen with golden threads the size of gillnetting, from an inexhaustable supply of golden twine?"

She must have just washed her hair because it was wet and hanging straight down. Like Henry's mother said, she was pretty. She smiled. She was in a good mood all the time, really, no matter what happened. And she didn't look the slightest bit put out to see the two of them standing there, even with Aaron talking in those riddles of his.

Aaron leaned up against the door jamb.

"Lend us your chainsaw, Eunice, your acetylene torch, your Honda generator, your welding mask, your rock chisels! Bring forth your hammers, your cutting tools, your cooling jets of water, your power thrusters!"

Henry Fiander just said, "Hi, Eunice."

"Come on in," said Eunice, "don't wake up the baby."

They went into the kitchen on tip-toe. They took their shoes off. Eunice put the kettle on and Aaron set out his plan, how he figured it, for the three of them.

"You got to be kidding. We don't own those fossils," said Eunice.

"Oh I think we do, it's the same as the berries out there," said Aaron. "You pick 'em, you sell 'em. Now, let's look at those tools, without which all our plans are nought."

Down they went to the basement. Eunice flicked on the light. There were the tools, lots of them lined up on the wall, hanging there on special hooks. They were so highly polished, light flashed off them, they glinted like silver plate.

"Look at that chainsaw," said Aaron Stoodley, "look at that, Henry. I could do anything with that, cut those fossils out of bare rock. Mind you, need a steady hand for that."

"Better off with a rock saw," said Eunice, "but we don't have one of those."

When she said those words, it was obvious that just like Henry Fiander had done earlier, Eunice Cluett had decided, okay, she'd throw her hand in too with Aaron Stoodley. Why not, what's to lose?

"Great, we'll start right in on the inventory tomorrow," said Aaron, "things go our way, it's a couple hundred thousand dollars by nightfall. We'll bring all those chisels too."

So it was that Henry and Aaron both left Eunice's feeling good about the plan they had, even though it was far-fetched, even though there was a ring around the full moon like a handcuff, even though the barometer started to fall as they slept. Worried fingers tapped the glass all along the Southern Shore. The marine forecast told fishermen, any of those that were left: stay home. And over in Baghdad, when it came down to it, despite the TV programme, very few of those poor Arabs were running off to Paris France for any sort of payday at all.

No matter. Next day, Henry was over to Aaron's early and he waited by the van they were going to use for the fossil run. He stood out of the wind, which was rising. He'd heard it start up in the middle of the night with an easy low moan and now the moan was more like a whistle, higher pitched. Aaron came out a few minutes later. His legs were so skinny, you could see his kneecaps through his jeans.

"Where we at for low tide?" asked Henry.

"Missed it, we'll make do," said Aaron Stoodley.

The original idea had been to sneak up on the fossils at the lowest tide possible. That way, there'd be lots of room on the rocks for the three of them, the crew. But low tide as it turned out was 3 a.m., in the middle of the night, so that part of the plan was overboard.

"Some wind this morning," said Henry.

"Lots of racket, sure," said Aaron, "but on the other hand, this is the best kind of weather for the chainsaw, my friend. No one hears a thing."

They picked up Eunice Cluett. She was dressed for the part all right. She had a lumberjack shirt on, and her coat said Cat Diesel Power over the left side of the chest. She was back in her ponytail again.

"Where's the baby?" said Henry.

"Up to Rhynie's for the day," she said.

Together they loaded up what they had. There was a chainsaw, lube oil, three large sledgehammers, a can of mix 20 to 1, and Eunice had those chisels of hers that still gleamed like money. Into the back of the van went the generator and the big torches and the welding mask, and off they went down the rock-and-dirt-and-gravel road due east, pitch-steep here and there, up and down in the gullies and washouts.

"Drive a new Buick out next time, Aaron Stoodley," Henry said.

"Why, sure, that'll be easy with the new funds," said Eunice, "all the black-market money. Maybe, Aaron Stoodley, you could buy a new set of jeans without holes."

"Hey, son of a gun, we're low on gas," said Aaron Stoodley, "damn, how'd that happen?"

It was no big deal to turn around, they'd only gone half-way.

"There goes another half hour by the tide," Henry said.

Ed, at the pumps, was surprised to see the three of them together.

"You okay, Eunice? What's up with these two?"

"Camping," she said.

Aaron went into the store, came out with some Cheesies and paid for the gas with what he called his nest egg for the endeavour, and again they started out in the van, back towards the Cape, and twenty minutes later they pulled over by the sign that said *Mistaken Point*.

They couldn't see the ocean; there was a dull roar out there to the south and there was mist in the air.

"They must have planted that sign real deep," said Eunice. "Otherwise she's gone."

In fact the wind was so strong, once they got out of the van, it was hard work to even stand up.

"Forget the heavy stuff in this," said Aaron. "We're going to have to travel light."

So Eunice took her lunch along and she carried the leather bag full of chisels, Henry took the gas and the oil, and Aaron had the Cheesies and he wouldn't let go of the chainsaw. Off they went into the blowing mist, peering into it.

"Lean and mean, see you there," said Aaron.

Off he went and then came Eunice and Henry. It was warm for October. The barrens were already red and brown all over. Aaron was so fast, he got out of earshot, whistling. His long legs ate up the yards. In another world and another time and with another personality, this would have been the perfect place for Henry to reach out and touch Eunice Cluett on the arm of her coat, and say something to her, something nice, something witty, something wry and something kind, and in that other world, she'd stop and put down those chisels and sweep the loose hair off her forehead and smile one of those smiles at him, a smile that said, "Okay, this is all right with me." But he didn't have it, that kind of smooth skill. He knew for him it would always be awkward, the stumbling word, the averted eye, and thus the missed opportunity.

But no, he actually said something.

"Eunice, come to the dance with me on Friday night?"

He shouted it over the wind. No way he could have said it in the normal fashion, he would have choked on it. Somehow though, when he shouted, the force of air in his lungs blew courage into him, and the words flew out of his mouth, surprised as he was.

"Fossils or no fossils, Eunice, either way," he shouted again.

All she did was walk on. She didn't hear a word. Or maybe she did, maybe she didn't.

Aaron then came back a bit, to hurry them up.

"We're getting close," he said.

The nearer they got to the shore, the higher blew the wind and it took Aaron's hair, and Henry's, and Eunice's, and blew it out straight back or across their eyes. It snatched their voices whenever they tried to talk. The roar from the shoreline was louder too, and the mist was more like rainfall, stinging sideways, salt water flying in on the gale. They huddled up closer together and walked up to the cliffside, holding onto all the tools they had.

There, the sea was so high it was hard to think straight.

Whoa, wait a minute, is what Henry thought, this is something else.

He stood where he was, fixed to the spot. Eunice didn't

seem to mind, but she didn't make a move down onto where the fossils were either. They all just stood there. It was only a little slide down, mostly grass, to the shale, maybe a six-foot drop. But they couldn't see enough to go forward, it was all black and grey and every time the surf hit further out it was like a firehose blown back.

Then all at once, "Let's move!" Aaron said.

He slid down the bank and crawled out onto the slick black table of streaming rock. He scuttled like a crab and kept low, with his head down. There went the Cheesies, they took off on their own and exploded against the cliffside and disappeared. Aaron Stoodley waved back, laughed, and pointed downwards. Then he was on his knees. Eunice and Henry both held their breath and slid on down like they were sea otters having a good time, except they weren't. Henry was close now to Eunice, who looked okay. Maybe the weight of the chisels held her faster on the rock, more secure than Henry felt with those damn fuel tanks that wobbled and cut into his hands. He should have left them up top, he figured. He put them down and cupped his hands around his eyes and looked at all the fossils lying there. How far from being an Arab could you get? Not much further, he figured. The leaves, the flowers, the fish, whatever they were, Henry thought, get me out of here, get us all out of here.

"Rev it up!" Aaron Stoodley said.

He was oblivious to it all. But they felt the boom of the ocean as another massive wave and then another piled through the wedge of rock that half-protected them from the sea. By now all of them were on their knees, but then Aaron stood up, put his feet wide apart, took a different kind of grip on the chainsaw, pulled the cord, and damn but it started right off.

"Baghdad!" he shouted.

Right away, Eunice and Henry jumped back cliffside to give him space and they watched him snap the chainbrake, rev the throttle and then he stood up, studied the rock floor as though he was one of those bearded professors, and then he leaned over and slammed the spinning teeth into the shale like he would have done with poplar.

He must have got blinded by the shower of sparks that exploded off the rock. He fell back, he stumbled twice, and there was no way he ever saw the giant wave which pounded down twice as heavy as any so far. It rose like a whiplash to Aaron's waist and, still holding the chainsaw, down he went, sucked right out like nothing in the backwash of that monster.

Like a speck in thunder, gone.

It took Eunice and Henry about four seconds to get back up on the meadow grass and run along to where they could see. By a miracle, he was still there, stuck and caught in one of those narrowed cracks that ran at right angles to the shore. Then the next wave came in, just as big as the last and Aaron disappeared again inside the white froth and tumble as it broke down on him, and they saw him, picked up by it and coming their way, shoreward. It was throwing him back like a piece of kelp torn off, and he still had the saw in his hand, dangling loose.

"Drop it, Aaron!" they shouted both at once but there was no way he could hear them. They couldn't hear themselves. He was thrown down by the force of the surge and he was barrel-rolled over the fossils in the rage of water that now came up to Henry's boots before it sucked back again. There was Aaron Stoodley flopped on the rocks. He looked dead. The chainsaw was gone. Without further thought, and later he wondered where that courage came from, Henry Fiander found himself in mid-air jumping towards the body, and Eunice was there too and they grabbed Aaron Stoodley by the collar and pulled him back up to the edge of the grass. He was a dead weight, water soaked through his clothes. He lay there blue and started to shake but he was alive. He moved his lips a bit but they couldn't hear what he said.

Maybe it was still "Baghdad."

Then the two of them took their dry coats off and piled them up on Aaron Stoodley to warm him up. That made it cold for them, but Eunice moved in tight to Henry, and to keep warm, she put her arm around his shoulders.

"Cold," she said.

He put his arm around her too, he lay it there as light as a feather, and then it was, right then, that it occurred to Henry that this was by far the best disaster he'd ever had. Even though, almost for sure, the reason Eunice Cluett was tucked in there the way she was, was because she lost her coat, because of the weather, because Aaron Stoodley was lying there half-way between the living and the dead. She was not there because she was in any way attracted or bonded to him for any reason, for any reason that would hold up for any longer than this one instant in time, this abnormal hypersituation that could never happen again even in another million years.

But he didn't ask why she did what she did. He just held onto her while he could, and the wind picked up again so that Eunice had to turn her face inwards, towards his neck, where her lips lay, where he could feel every warm breath she took.

Then Eunice broke off the hold she had. She pulled her head back from his shoulder and she looked at him with her blue eyes directly into his face. She held that look for a long long time and then, despite the cold, she stood up and grabbed her bag of tools and slid on back down to where the fossils were. This time she stayed up real high. There was a lull in the waves and the weather, the kind of lull that always happens when you're there long enough, and she took advantage of it. She took out one of those shiny chisels of hers, and a hammer, and around one of those animals, or plants, it was hard to tell which, she chipped away for maybe ten minutes, real careful and slow. The edges broke and cracked some, but when the piece came away, it was perfect.

She gave it to Aaron Stoodley when he woke up.

"There," she said, "we got it."

Then they all went home.

It turned out that none of them made any money at all, not even from that one chipped-out fossil. It never got anywhere near Paris, France. Instead, Aaron Stoodley put it up at home, on the mantle next to the picture of the Pope, a picture that someone— it must have been Aaron—had, one time in the past, taken out of its silver frame and, with a magic marker, replaced the usual ivory-white raiments with the exact replica of a knitted sweater, all in bright yellow. That particular Pope, the one with the yellow sweater, he looked good. He looked warm. The chipped-out fossil lay beside him on the mantle as though it were a simple home decoration.

Aaron, Henry, Eunice, none of them were interested in selling it. It had way too much sentimental value. It was a personal souvenir of the time Aaron Stoodley floated out onto the ocean like a wood chip and came back alive, of the time Eunice was still a single mother, of the time that Henry and Eunice sat shivering with their arms around each other.

Henry got home that night and remembered, amazed, that he'd asked her out to the Legion dance. She'd given no indication she'd heard a thing. He'd shouted into the wind with all the courage he could muster, and been greeted with silence.

When they looked back on it, they saw that luck had touched them all out there at Mistaken Point. Not in the obvious way, in the way that no one had died, that Aaron Stoodley had been thrown back alive, that the only thing lost was a chainsaw. No, it was more than that.

Luck had flown through the spray and the mist and the savage waves and laid like a wreath on their shoulders. On Henry's shoulders, most of all. That's what he felt. When Eunice Cluett breathed upon his neck the way she did, it was the first indication he'd ever had that his life, such as it was, could someday be etched in stone like those fossils, that he wouldn't be scattered piecemeal, that he could screw up his courage, knock on her door at seven on Friday night, carry Queenie to her aunt's, walk to the Legion with Eunice Cluett, hand in hand the whole way. Dance all night.

Not bad at all, not bad at all, Mistaken Point.

shuffle

IT MUST HAVE been some other place you learned to slow dance like this, to breathe in such a space so tight, rapt, oblivious, still moving though the music's stopped, the band stepping down, it's break time, walk to the parking lot, why not, look west, the sun's fading behind the hill called Blue Pinion, and look what the night wind has done, it's ruffled your hair, pulled at the corner of your blouse, twisted your skirt just so; we can say anything at all, feel the dark breeze shuffle through.

how eunice got her baby

EUNICE CLUETT DIDN'T get her baby, Queenie, in the usual way, through sexual intercourse with a boy in a bed, in a car, or out on the meadow after dark. Instead, she inherited her baby from the estate of her older sister, Florence, through a tragedy. From the estate? Well, it wasn't really an estate, because of course there was no will made up, but when the baby became available, through the sudden accident that claimed the life of Florence, it was Eunice who was first in line. And that was a proper thing as it turned out, because Eunice was the best mother a baby could have. Better than the natural mother, some said, because Florence had a wild way about her that Eunice didn't have. Flo was impulsive and did things on a dare. Flo drove down the Trans-Canada Highway on the blackest night of the year with all the car lights turned off so she could see the stars better. Flo shut her eyes, or pretended to shut her eyes, and she crossed the busiest streets like that, with her arms stretched out.

"Look at me," she said. "I'm a zombie."

She also drank way too many beers too early on at dances, then right away she'd dance too close, and stay out way too late, past the wee hours. She skipped classes at school the next day too, including the ones on precautions, and how she got her baby was therefore no mystery to any of her friends. Why, more often than not, Flo came home with her underpants scrunched up in her purse.

That was Flo, but that was not Eunice, and that's how her little baby, Pasquena, who they all called Queenie, got lucky, sort of, when tragedy struck her mother down.

Now let's not go on too much about the wild side of Flo. There was lots that was good about her. "She's got energy to burn," that's what her father said, whenever he was asked. "She's got her thermostat cranked up high."

Her father talked like that because he had one of the best jobs on the whole Southern Shore, and that involved fuel oil. He had a yellow truck everybody recognized, and he knew everything there was to know about thermostats, and energy, and the foolish waste of heat. Some families burned their oil up twice as fast as others, he'd seen that over and over. And Flo?

"Well, Flo, she's like a comet," he said, "there's no stopping Flo. She's fire in the sky. She burns oil."

She was the oldest of all the seven children, the first in line, the experimental one, and Eunice was the baby, the last of the whole family. That meant, praise the Lord, that Eunice got insulated from the wild side of Flo by nine whole years, and all she knew about Flo was the love and the care she got from the only sister she had. Eunice always got a kiss, nothing less, no matter how late Flo got home, no matter how scrunched up Flo's underpants might have been, pushed into the top of her purse just a half hour before. Eunice got the kisses, but she never dreamed she'd get a baby from Flo. If she'd ever dreamed that, it would have been a nightmare. There's not too many good ways you can inherit a baby.

Even with Flo being the way she was, everything would have

been fine if it hadn't been for the boy she met. His name was Darryl Bugden, and though he had lots of charms and attributes attractive to a girl, he also had the heart and the spirit of a criminal born. Not just one who picked it up along the way, for a lark with friends, but one born right to it from the word go.

How'd it happen? Flo was at the Minimart, the one she worked at on Long's Hill, reading a magazine and sitting by the cash, when she was introduced to Darryl. There was no one else in the store. It was 8 p.m., three hours to go before she closed up against the scattered few customers who came in. It was mostly cigarettes and chips and the furtive magazines for total losers, that's all.

"This here's a stick-up," was what Darryl said, his first words to her.

Flo looked up and there he was, six foot four at least, with dark curly hair and a smile despite what he said to her. All those teeth were perfect.

What's with that, she thought, perfect teeth? That's rare.

He did not look threatening to Flo, but how could she know, that death would appear to her in this outfit, those teeth, those words she'd only heard on TV? It never occurred to her, and it never would have occurred to anyone, looking at that smile. Anyway, it sure didn't happen right away, it took three years.

"A stick-up?" she said.

When she got the job, the boss said to her, "If someone comes in and says, this is a stick-up, then you just collapse to the floor in a dead faint. Piss your pants too, that's the best. Make as big a mess as you can, breathe like you're a spastic on the verge of a fit. Oftentimes they'll just say, Jesus Christ!, and run out of the store and go somewhere else."

Somehow the boss had figured that out on his own, from what happened to him once. He didn't plan it, it just happened to him and it worked. He sure didn't get that advice out of the manual that came to all the new employees, from the Downtown Merchants. In that manual, it said, just hand over all the money, wordless, and do not put up any resistance. Most of these robbers are on drugs and they're twitchy, unpredictable.

It was the nice smile he had that kept her sitting there. There was no way she was going to fall to the floor and do the rest of that whole crazy drill. How bad could a girl look, no matter what?

"There's no money here. Everything bigger than a five goes right down that slot," she said.

She pointed to the wall behind her.

"Straight down into the safe."

Actually it was a slot in the wall that went straight into a cardboard liquor box that was on top of the safe. She could see it in her mind's eye, sitting there full of loose money spilling over the sides. The boss long ago forgot the number to the safe so this was a money bypass. "It's a trick," he said, "that fools most of them all the time."

"The safe, the combination is unknown to me," she said.

He smiled some more but he just stood there.

"The walls are three feet thick, and solid iron," she said.

The next thing Darryl did was get over the counter. He suddenly turned and slid his butt over the plexiglass that lay over top of the lottery tickets, and there he was, he twisted around and his feet landed on the floor right beside Flo. They stood there like a couple. She got scared then, and looked out the door. Maybe there'd be a customer to come in and save her, but that was not likely, maybe the old man with the cane or the fat lady for bubble gum, but what chance of that? There was no one in sight. And what chance would they have, her hopeless customers, anyway?

None, she figured.

"Lay down on the floor," he said.

Those were the next words he had with the love of his life.

Down went Flo onto the linoleum. The tiles were lifted here and there, swept just once a week so they didn't raise the dust, and she knew her white blouse, the one she bought with her own money, the one she never should have worn that night, would be ruined. Thank God for the old jeans she had on. Maybe she'd be dead soon enough anyway. It wouldn't matter then what she had on, unless there was a picture in the paper. They didn't usually show dead bodies. Even then, so what? Flo didn't care about that, really.

Then she lost her nerve all at once.

"There there, don't cry," said Darryl, "just shut up."

Then Darryl took his left foot and laid it down on Flo's chest near her throat while she lay there in the dirt. It was a boot like a cowboy might have, with a heel like iron maybe two inches long.

"I'm now the man at the cash tonight," he said.

He pressed his foot on her throat some, but she could still breathe.

"Don't you say a word or move, or I'll stomp on your windpipe with the toe of this boot. They got steel toes."

There was a tinkle from the doorbell and she heard the shuffle-shuffle of the old man with the cane. Eight fifteen on the button every night, for the newspaper and the dog food. Once the boss saw that the old man always got dog food, he'd marked up the cans to $2.00 for each and every one.

"The old guy will never notice that," he said, "the old goat, the old geezer, the old fool."

Later, Flo changed it back to $1.25 with the rotating stamp.

The boss'll never notice that, she said to herself, the old miser.

That was the general atmosphere at the Minimart, so Darryl there behind the counter, his foot on Flo's throat, didn't really change things all that much.

"Where's Flo?" said the old man when he came up to pay.

"Underfoot somewhere, maybe in the back," said Darryl bold as brass. "I'm on the cash tonight. For all I know, she's lying down somewhere."

HOW EUNICE GOT HER BABY

That's how the rest of the night was with Darryl. Flo lay on the floor but she couldn't cry anymore. Darryl took in all the cash and put none of it down the slot. After an hour went by, Darryl took off his boots with the steel toes and just pressed on her neck with his stocking foot. She was surprised, the sock smelled clean, like wool. Whenever she looked up, he still had on that smile which never changed. He thought he was a smart-ass, she could tell, but that was common enough in all the men she knew. By nine thirty, she no longer trembled but Darryl was none too happy with the lousy take of, so far, $38.50.

"This is one slow store," Darryl said.

That foot of his seemed to move further down from her throat, down her chest until it was right on the top of her left breast. She shifted down a bit.

"Not a lot of money comes in to this dumb store," he said.

"Watch that foot please," said Flo.

"Sorry," said Darryl.

He released a bit of pressure but he didn't shift the toes at all.

"Is that better?"

"That's better."

In the quiet times, between the customers, Flo thought she could feel his foot getting rhythmic on her chest.

Oh well, just lay there, she figured, let it go.

"I might just close up early," said Darryl at 10:30.

"Leave now," said Flo, "there's an idea."

"Then what do I do with you?"

"Me?"

"You're the eye witness."

"The eye witness?"

Oh no, she thought, this could come to a nasty turn now. Her heart began to thump so hard, under that foot on her blouse, that she thought, for sure, this guy could feel it there, thumping under his wandering toes. There was no doubt where that foot was now.

"You're the only eye witness to this crime," Darryl said, "my crime."

He smiled down at Flo.

"I wonder, what should I do with you, girl?"

"All those people saw you too, that came and went," she said.

"None of them that I saw had any kind of brain to remember," he said.

Then Flo found the way out that saved her in the short run but in the long run, it didn't make that much difference.

"Ask me what I saw tonight," she said,

She looked up at Darryl from the floor and willed that heart of hers to stop that dreadful pounding noise it made.

"Okay, what?"

"I saw this guy, maybe five foot seven, a thin guy with rotten teeth and a weasel face who came in and robbed the store and held me down on the floor with a gun, the whole time, and took all the money that came in until you came in and chased him off."

"I did that?"

"You were brave."

"I was brave like a lion."

"Yes, you were."

"Then what happened?"

"He ran away down the hill."

"Like a rabbit."

"Mind moving that foot please to the other side?"

"Like that?"

"That's better. Yes. That's a lot better."

"How's that feel?"

"That feels better, it feels good."

The bad part was, she wasn't lying when she said that.

"You saved my life. You paid for smokes, you looked over the counter, you're tall, you saw me on the floor and you said to the guy, what's with the girl on the floor? And it was then that he pulled out his gun, forced you up against the rack of chips, and then he slipped out the door and ran and ran. You stayed with me. We made the call."

As she lay there, Florence could see the little man with the bad teeth running and running down Long's Hill, the lights from the passing cars flashing off his legs, the sound of his footsteps getting smaller and smaller.

"What's your name?" Darryl said.

"Florence."

"Florence, you get up now."

He reached down and gave her a hand up and dusted her off. He spent a lot of time on the blouse and on the upper parts of the jeans, where they were the dustiest.

Then, together, they put in the call to the Constabulary, and together they told the same story they'd worked on, as if they were old friends. Then they went out to George Street and drank up the money that Darryl had made that night.

One thing led to another. They were both reckless to a fault. One day, it was too late for Florence, she'd missed three periods, maybe four, and little Queenie was on the way, unstoppable.

The doctor said to her, "I'm sorry, Florence, there's no way, you're too far along for anything but to carry on with this little baby."

That was okay with Flo. By then, she loved Darryl in her way, despite that smile he always had.

Her friends all warned her, "Look at that guy, Flo, that smile of his."

That was the worst thing they said. Darryl could be happy, sad, busy or bored, or mean, nasty as anything, and it was always the same, his smile. Sure it was handsome, winsome even to a foolish girl, but it was a sick smile, forever as empty as his stupid criminal heart was of anything like kindness.

"Look out, Florence," they said.

But she never listened. She never saw it that way. It must have been how he put the sock on her chest that night, the knowledge he had from being older, like Flo was some kind of hostage all her life one way or another, underfoot, in the way.

The writing was on the wall, the late-night driving they did up and down the Number 10 Highway, the open beers that rolled on the floor, all the shady stuff that Darryl pulled, including the final trip that had something to do with crystal meth, the Winnebago that lumbered over the centre line with Darryl half-dazed, the old guy at the wheel, all that momentum they both built up when they hit. The front grill of the Winnebago went straight head-on through Darryl's rusted-up Chevrolet and it took the motor of that car, in one big jangled piece, slam-back through that smirk of his, and right through Florence too, until they all ended up in the trunk, fused and welded together by the flames that broke out, probably from the cigarette that Darryl always had to have, hanging there from his lip.

That's how Eunice inherited her baby, from her sister, Flo, by accident.

Flo had come by earlier that day and left Queenie with her, like she'd had some kind of premonition. She was a good mother, really, when you got down to it.

"Here," Flo had said, "take Queenie a bit. Darryl and me, we're off to where there's no place for a girl."

You really can't get much better than that, when it comes to mothering.

strait

I learned a song in Margaree.
It rang inside my head:
Wrap me up in dungaree,
This morning I am dead.

THE CANSO CAUSEWAY was built in 1952 between the low mainland of Nova Scotia and the hills of Cape Breton Island and it took ten million tons of granite blasted from the face of Cape Porcupine to do it, the ocean breached and the ferry service gone like that; it was the lifeline but also the blood-letting of music, the time of strathspeys who took it upon themselves to be the first to step out upon the roadbed ginger-haired, and in the peace that followed upon this no-man's-land excursion into the more-solid world, a stream of reels giddied down upon the steam of asphalt laid there by the yellow machines that called out jobs for us, the trucks, the wheels the size of boulders strewn by the same shake-up in the landscape of green, the morning clouds of jagged rock, the reels impetuous but off to a late start from the night before, slurred and graced and staccato'd into air still tanged up with the vapour blows of oil and diesel and the shouts of the gulls who multiplied with all the fuss, like showgirls they were that fluttered on the flow of the whitecaps now divided by the rubble that lay there S-shaped from shore to shore, and the workmen pounded in the guardrails for the slow airs to insinuate upon, which they did, the breath-notes twined in and out and stayed there as locked in time as any simple thought you ever had, vanguarding for the slip-jigs that then came down, rockets and flares in 9/8 time, their sixteenth- and thirty-second notes shredded and torn and flung from Bras d'Or high up there in the thunderstorms of August, the ozone heavy in the air, the line painters, the man with the steady hand who had to wait for the weather to change, the ribbon cut, the banshee cry, the wild scratch of horsehair whipped from the stammered bow, the fiddler himself anguished and stepped-out, the keening, back-lit kilted traditional furious pummelling of notes that rolled on down the Causeway, now unimpeded by the Strait surpassed, straight past all of us to the downtown city of New York.

scenario 2 a.m.

AARON STOODLEY COULDN'T get the botulism party out of his head. All of those distant relatives of his, dead and gone, just three weeks after Mistaken Point. Sure, he inherited nine thousand dollars from the disaster, and that changed his life a little bit. But nighttimes, he'd find himself wondering about the party, how it happened. He started to make up what he called scenarios, to fill in the blanks.

"None of it, Henry," he said, "bothered me in any way. Totally detached, I was."

But there he found himself at 2 a.m., he couldn't sleep, and he ran through it in his head like a movie, scene after scene, imagining it all from scratch, seeing how easy it was for everything to slip away.

First he saw the dog, the little fox terrier, and in one scenario the dog was asleep in the apartment, all by himself. There was a radiator under the window, and that was where the little dog slept all day, on a raggy blue blanket. There was an empty bowl sitting there for kibble. Now and then, the little dog got up and growled at nothing. It tugged and pulled away at the edge of the blanket with its teeth. Then a pigeon flew by and landed on the outside, up on the windowsill, and the fox terrier jumped up and barked and the pigeon flew away.

"It flew away like the passing of a spirit," said Aaron Stoodley.

He had another scenario which showed the same room, but this time there was no dog. The blue blanket was there, and so was the radiator, but the pigeon perched up on the windowsill for a long time. *Coo-coo-coo* it went, and that was the only sound you could hear because the apartment was empty. It was the middle of the afternoon, a lot of light came in from the window.

Next thing that happened, in both scenarios, were footsteps on the stairs and the front door opened. Then either the fox terrier jumped up from the blanket and ran to the door, or the fox terrier came in on a leash from the outside. Either way, the scene was set and Aaron liked it better when he pictured it the first way, the dog all alone in the house for such a long time.

Then the six people who lived there came inside, all of them together. They were dressed up in their soccer uniforms, they were a team. Falcons, was what it said on the front of the shirts, and there were numbers, all different, on the back. They all laughed and clumped straight into the kitchen, took off their soccer shoes, pushed them into a pile.

"They spent the rest of their lives in just their socks," Aaron said.

First through the door was Otto Bond and then in came Johnny Drake. Johnny Drake put a carton of beer on the floor. Then he filled up the refrigerator with the beer bottles, one by one. He had one open already, it looked like he didn't care if it was warm or maybe they'd bought it cold, refrigerated. Aaron wasn't sure. Then in came the others. Terry Snook, Shawn Blagdon, Barry Rose, and Justin Peach. Aaron rhymed off the names like that. He knew them all from the lawyer's papers, from the inheritance, from the stories in the newspapers.

Otto Bond was stocky, he had his hair cut short and he was the quickest soccer player you ever seen. They won the men's championship that night.

"All Halifax," said Aaron.

That was the truth all right. He'd read it in the *Daily News*, read what the police found when they came in, later on.

It was Otto Bond who owned the dog and you could tell he liked it. First he took the dog out to the park. Then he came back and he went over and got out some kibble from the cupboard, put it into the bowl and shook it, so it made a sound. The dog came over and snuffed at it, but you could tell that he'd had a awful lot of kibble before.

"Oh, eat the food, doggy-oh," sang Otto Bond.

Then the boys got hungry and the dog was up on the couch curled up in one lap or another. There were no girls there at all. That meant the six of them concentrated on laughing and hooting and joking, just being themselves.

Six, seven o'clock came around and by then they were all in the livingroom. There was a couch, a TV, and a bean-bag chair. Three of them sat on the floor on a rag-rug from home. There was a picture woven into that rug, the *S.S. Caribou*, the ship full of innocent passengers that the Germans sank with a torpedo back in 1942. Down it went, the *Caribou* ship, down to the bottom off Port-aux-Basques. Hundreds drowned. Trouble was, Aaron saw in his scenario, the rag-rug was so old and so twisted out of shape, the ship bent here and there in the fabric, it looked like an old wreck even before the torpedo hit.

That said, it was still afloat on the sea, smoke from the funnels.

"It was an omen too then, the rug, like the pigeon," Henry Fiander said.

"That's right," said Aaron Stoodley, "you could say that."

Now he had that old carpet at home, part of the inheritance.

About once a month, in Halifax, Otto Bond had taken the *S.S.*

Caribou rug outside and shook off all the crumbs. Then it was nice to sit on, and three of the boys sat there on the championship night.

"What'd they look like, physically?" Henry asked.

"They were all different, I bet, but in my mind's eye, at least one of them bore a certain resemblance to my grandmother, Priscilla."

It was through the connection to Priscilla Yarn that Aaron came by the money. Therefore someone must have looked a bit like Priscilla, or her long-dead husband.

It was that Justin Peach who came up with the idea that caused them all to die.

"Let's order in," he said, "pizza."

That's how simple it was. They could have decided to go out, they could have had anything they wanted served up. Instead they ordered in, and it was Otto Bond who said, "I'll do it, let me do it, I'll call."

"Hold the cod-liver oil," they heard him say.

"Might come over later," Bridie whispered over the phone, "but it kind of depends on Mother."

"Oh?"

"They might need her at the Legion, they might not. I'll let you know, Otto Bond."

Bridie's mother had to work overtime so Bridie missed the party and after it all happened, and was over with, she consoled herself as best she could, in the middle of her episodes of crying, she said to baby Liam, "Oh my stars!" and she cuddled up with him.

"You were almost an orphan, my little darling. Wouldn't that have been a fine state of affairs?"

Years later, she still thought about Otto Bond on a regular basis, because she knew he was the best of all the boyfriends she ever had. He was the gold standard.

Justin Peach did it again. While Otto was still on the phone with Bridie, he came over and tapped Otto on the shoulder.

"Hey! Order a couple empty blank pizza crusts too, we got that sauce of mine," he said.

So, when the pizzas were delivered, there were those three empty crusts that Justin Peach fixed up. He went out of sight from the livingroom, into the kitchen, and it took him a long, long time. He banged around, you could hear the pots and pans. When he came back in, he looked so proud, no one knew they were looking at their last supper.

"Jeez, Justin Peach, what you got on there?" they all said.

Aaron Stoodley could see him there plain as day. Justin Peach stood with his own home-made pizza and held it up, slanted, so they could see it. Steam rose up it was so hot.

"You're gonna love this," he said, "got my own tomato sauce boiled up, sat in the fridge a bit, seasoned it up. Cod tongues and cheeks. Side order, chips and gravy."

Now that sounded good. After the soccer game, the victory and the beer, they had plenty of room for the Justin Peach Special. That's what they called it, and they ate it all down but for a piece or two.

"That's what did it, what killed them," Aaron said. "It was the sauce."

The little dog wandered around about for five or six hours and sniffed at a couple of slices that were left over. But he was too smart, he turned his nose up and walked away, ate a bit of his dry kibble, *crunch-crunch*, and he looked at the boys, puzzled, every one of them now dead to the world.

Aaron said he was detached, emotionally, but he knew how the dog must have felt.

"Lucky loved them, every single one," he said.

He'd named the dog Lucky himself, later on.

"I think we might've been buddies with Otto Bond, Henry, but we never had the chance. None of them knew a damn thing about botulism."

"Botulism?"

All of a sudden, Aaron Stoodley was the leading world expert on all the poisons you could get, cooked into food. He told Henry how he saw it in his scenario, how he saw it clear as day.

Johnny Drake was the first to go because he had most of the beer. He had a head start on the rest of them, he felt weak on his legs. He'd never felt his lips go numb like that, and never before saw double. Now he saw two of the little dogs, so he lay down, tried to orient his eyes, lay back so he was part-way in the bean-bag chair, part-way on the floor, his legs stretched out, and he breathed real shallow for a couple of hours.

"Could have laid a feather on his lips," said Aaron, "but he never woke up. Last thing he saw was a loon on the water. It opened up its mouth, voiceless."

Then the botulism that was hidden in the sauce caught up to Terry Snook. He was out on the wharf with his sister when she ran home for lunch and left him there. He heard a low sound, like a make-and-break engine miles away, a choking off and on.

Shawn Blagdon? He went out for a walk, out when the tide was low and when he looked back there was nothing behind him but water. Couldn't swim a bit, gave up easy. Barry Rose walked up Iron Skull, he liked to do that, it took all day to climb the mountain that looked over the sea, and when he got to the top the wind died real mysteriously. He couldn't see half-way to English Harbour.

Aaron Stoodley was too upset at Justin Peach to figure out just what went on, what it was that Justin Peach saw when he died.

"That fool Justin Peach," said Aaron, "he'd cooked up that sauce way back when, he'd mixed it in a pan like it was just beans for dinner. Never thought of the pressure cooker, didn't know a damn thing about fixing up preserves. Once, maybe twice, he put up jam."

Aaron Stoodley would have given back the nine thousand dollars just to have those boys alive, have them wake up, but they never did.

Of course the last one to go on that night was the soccer star himself, Otto Bond. He lay back and his blonde hair, what there was of it, cut real short, was bent up against the arm of the couch from the weight of his head. He felt his mouth go dry. He saw Bridie from the pizza place. Then he saw the winning goal go in again, curled off his foot up high, smack up under the crossbar.

He saw the little baby in her arms.

Then he felt the dog jump on his lap and that was the last thing he knew, and the dog was still there when the police came and broke down the door, and by that time Otto Bond was cold. He felt like he was made out of porcelain, when they touched him.

Aaron didn't have to make up any scenarios after that. It was all in the newspapers in Halifax. Public knowledge, how the boys from the soccer team died overnight. The terrier had his picture in the paper, ONLY SURVIVOR it said underneath in capital letters, and off he went to the SPCA. He was still there six months later when in came Aaron Stoodley, re-named him Lucky and brought him home to stay. That's how long it took, six months no less, for the lawyers from Halifax to track down Aaron. They gave him all the money the boys had, what there was of it. It didn't amount to much, especially after the lawyers, but Aaron was the closest living relative they had left on the earth, so he was the one to get it.

Still, Aaron Stoodley couldn't sleep at night. The nine thousand dollars, the dog named Lucky, the rag-rug, he had them all, but when he looked in the mirror, he saw his face was worn, his arms and legs got all sagged out like he was a hundred years old.

"Total insomnia, I've got it bad," he said to Henry Fiander.

Henry watched him fall apart for a month or two and then, after talking to Eunice Cluett, he gave him some considered advice.

"Snap out of it, Aaron Stoodley, smarten up, you got your whole life to think of."

It couldn't have been that simple admonition that did it, but the next day Aaron looked a lot better.

"What happened to you?" Henry asked.

"I had another scenario, and I fell asleep."

Then he told Henry what he saw. First off, he realized—thank God, Henry—that what happened was that Otto Bond didn't die after all. Sure, he was taken to the morgue in the same ambulance as Terry Snook. Aaron saw it, the ambulance had a red cross on its side, no siren, after all what's the rush, so it pulled in slowly, carefully, under a stone arch by the hospital and it stopped and then the back doors opened up. A couple of men in white uniforms appeared and took out the stretchers. You couldn't see the boys at all because they were covered up in sheets, like ghosts. Then the men in the uniforms wheeled the carts down a long hall and turned into a room.

My, but it was cold in there.

They lifted Terry Snook and they lifted Otto Bond and they placed them just as they were on a metal table. One metal table for each. All six of them then, all the friends, were there lined up in a row. Then the men left and turned off the light and it got colder and colder in the pitch-black dark.

If it hadn't been for the night cleaner, whose name was Moses Sealy, Otto Bond would have died again for sure, frozen to death. As it was, it took a couple of hours until Moses came in. He turned on the overhead light so he could see around. He swept up the floor with a broom. He had on a big pair of green rubber gloves, so he didn't have to touch anything, and he didn't seem at all worried by the boys being there. Then Moses Sealy finished up, flicked off the light, started to go out the door and then for some reason he turned back and turned the light on again.

Hey that sheet's moving, Moses thought to himself.

Prickles ran up and down his spine. He looked again and sure enough there was a motion of breathing there. You could scarcely see it. He walked over, slipped off one of his gloves, pulled the white sheet down off Otto Bond's head.

This boy's not so cold. Feel him.

He took off his other glove, went to the wall phone, called 9-1-1, and he sat right down beside Otto Bond till they got there.

After two weeks on the respirator in Intensive Care, after they heated him up with electric blankets, Otto Bond walked out as good as new. Except he had weak legs. First thing though, he went down to the pizza place. Bridie fainted when she saw him, and Jules picked her off the floor and told her to go home with Otto Bond. Then the two of them walked over to Bridie's, got the baby into the stroller, met Bridie's mother for the first time.

"Pleased to meet you, Otto Bond," is what she said.

Her mother liked him right off, you could see it, the way she acted the whole time when he was there.

Later she said to Bridie, "Oh my, I do likes him, Bridie, he seems like a fine boy."

Aaron Stoodley told Henry and Eunice it was then that he fell asleep, by a miracle. He figured it was about 2 a.m. that it happened. When he woke up, he felt rested; he had the little dog, Lucky, curled up half-way down his feet.

fog

IT WAS A busy day and a lucky one for them, the day they ran over Aaron Stoodley in the fog. They could have killed him but they didn't, just by accident got involved in the event that turned his life around. It even gave them, Henry and Eunice, a leg up too, as it turned out.

It was a Monday, so Queenie and Henry and Eunice had to get up early. Eunice had the job—she did the laundry down at the nursing home. There was a lot of drooling there, and worse, so Eunice went in part-time. Turn-around time on the sheets, the towels, the washcloths was critical, according to Mrs. Hann. She could lose her license. So even though the visibility outside was down to zero, off they had to go. The rain was hanging out there like a shroud. Little Queenie materialized out of the mist like a mummer, held her shiny black purse with the gold chain out in front of her. You wouldn't know the ocean was anywhere, it was so quiet.

They drove real slowly, to keep out of trouble. Henry could barely see the ornament on the hood, and all the wipers did was move the water off till it layered up again.

As usual, it was Queenie's job to spot the stop signs. Two years old, but she was smart, dependable. If she didn't shout out "Stop Sign," he'd drive right through like he was stunned. He had it all figured out, which made it perfectly safe. He stared straight ahead, looked out of the side of his eyes without moving them at all. All you got to do if you want to try it sometimes, is raise your eyebrows.

They'd all laugh when he did that, it made the seventeen miles into town seem like nothing at all. There were only two of those stop signs before the yellow flasher downtown, and when Queenie shouted out "Stop Sign," Henry would stop right off and say, "Oh my God thank you, Pasquena, if it hadn't been for you we'd have gone through that stop sign."

And Eunice would say, "Good for you, Queenie."

They were used to fog, thick fog off the Grand Banks. It was a fact of life. Henry learned to drive long ago by the feel of the Goodyears; he wove his way back and forth ever so slightly from the blacktop to the shoulder, he felt the gravel kick up under the floorboards, turned back again to the pavement, snaked up and down the right side of the road. They kept the radio off so they could hear and feel the sound of the gravel kicking up.

Ten miles an hour, tops.

"Stop sign!"

Sure enough there it was off the right fender. Queenie was quick, even after forty minutes of nothing. Seven more miles, that meant.

Henry put on the brakes and came to a nice little stop.

"Oh my God, thank you, Pasquena," he said.

"Queenie, good for you," said Eunice.

They started back up again.

"Maybe, Eunice, ask for a raise? Seven dollars an hour, we'd at least pay for gas."

"I know. We got to go west, Henry, I think, the tar sands."

"Alberta? I don't know about that, that means a ferry ride. Could make Queenie sick."

Henry had once been on the Fortune to St. Pierre ferry on a rough day. There'd been a lot of heavers on that trip, and to tell the truth, he got queasy himself. One guy by the rail had berry pie and carrots stuck in his beard. He should never have looked windward when he threw up his lunch. Sometimes it just happens though, it catches you unawares.

"Stop sign!"

No sign of let-up in the fog.

"Queenie, you're some sharp. Now watch for the turn-in."

One hundred yards now to the Fiddler's Green Rest Home, best guess. Henry relaxed but kept the car at a crawl. It was a damn nice situation, the heater was kicked in, the three of them were happy, solid as could be. Still no sign of the yellow flasher though. All of a sudden Henry felt a thump somewhere near where Eunice sat, and then there was this bump, a kind of soft jar, they all felt it. It came up through the front right tire.

"Jeez, what was that?"

He stopped the car dead. The rear wheel hadn't bumped up yet.

"I saw nothing out there," said Eunice.

"A moose, a bear?" said Henry.

"Something, that's for sure."

They sat there and they listened.

"Eunice, you hear something?"

"Aaron Stoodley," Queenie said.

"No," said Eunice, "quiet, don't say anything. Listen."

There. Henry thought he could hear a moan. He wasn't sure. There was still no sign of wind, nothing out there to make a sound like that.

"Jeez," he said, "I don't know."

"Henry, get out of the car."

"Eunice, just open your window first, take a look down."

Henry knew a trucker who hit a bull moose on the Trans-Canada near Gander, got out to investigate and then bang, his friend got skewered through and through by the rack of the moose. Mind you, that animal was dead, his neck was snapped and broken on impact, but the nervous system was still alive, the antlers kicked and thrashed on their own. Struck poor Mr. John Fudge right through the heart and he bled to death right there. The

FOG

Mounties had to close the highway, call in the clean-up crew. They had to use Industrial Dust-Bane, that's what Henry heard.

Eunice rolled her window down.

"Can't see a thing."

She was leaning half-way out of the car by then, her jeans lifted right off the vinyl.

For sure a kind of low-pitched groaning sound came from what seemed to be just under the middle of the stalled car. It didn't sound like a wild animal.

"Eunice, Queenie, I'm getting out now."

It had to be done. For safekeeping, he popped out the keys and gave them to Eunice. He left the headlights on just in case, but he didn't want to get blinded so he went around in the red glow of the back fender, feeling his way alongside the car, sidling through the fog like he was Sherlock Holmes. Carefully, he stepped up to the passenger side. Then his boots hit something soft and the softness moaned out.

"Henry," it said.

"Oh Jeez, Aaron Stoodley. You're no bloody moose."

He was lying there at right angles to the car, just under where Eunice sat. His skinny legs were half-under and in the backwash from the lights you could see the tire prints on his overalls, round about the knees. They'd run him over sure enough, but they'd missed his head, his vitals.

Eunice opened up her door.

"Hey Eunice," Aaron Stoodley said, "help me."

Henry bent down. Aaron must have been outside for some time before they bumped over him. His woolen coat was sodden through.

Eunice then stepped out her door, and, blinded by the mix of fog and lights, she brought her boot and her weight down by accident on Aaron's lower stomach.

"Oh my," Aaron said.

His legs bent up all of a sudden till they were stopped by the bottom of the car.

"Eunice, he's moving those legs just fine!" said Henry.

Things were beginning to look up.

"Let's pull him out from under now," said Eunice. "Queenie, don't you go too far away."

Queenie had gotten out of the car too. She was bent down playing in the grass, in the ditch grass, putting pebbles in her purse.

Eunice and Henry took an armpit each and pulled Aaron Stoodley out from under the car. They were careful, like first-aiders. Then they bent him up ninety degrees at the waist and they watched him work his legs real slow, up and down, flexing his knees. There was no blood anywhere. They half-lifted him, half-pushed him and sat him up against the back door. His head was kind of lolling around like one of those rear-window travelling dogs.

"Stand up, Aaron Stoodley!"

That was Eunice. She'd had enough, and now she was late for work.

"Put him in the back, Henry, sort of fold him up."

They bent him double and Eunice got the back door open and they slid him in.

"Queenie! Get in the car, pronto," said Eunice.

Henry took the keys back from Eunice, revved her up and eased down gently on the accelerator and then it was finally through the yellow flasher and there they were at the Fiddler's Green. Eunice got out with her ponytail, and though Henry couldn't see it for the fog, he knew that Mrs. Hann would be right there to say hello. The first few times, when Eunice first went to work, Mrs. Hann waited by the frosted doors—the ones you couldn't see through—and said, "Miss Cluett, it's ten seconds to eight o'clock."

Now they were friends. She'd backed off watching like a hawk.

So there they were, just Queenie and Henry and the run-over Aaron Stoodley. Aaron obviously needed to be warmed up so they went to the Trepassey Inn for a cup of tea. They opened early there because, for the owners, there was nothing better to do. A perfect place, really, for customers. Aaron was like a cripple up the steps but they landed him safe and sound at the first table. Henry ordered green Jello for Queenie, which made her happy right off. They hung Aaron's coat up on a hook beside the table, and they watched it drip, start puddles on the floor.

"Aaron, that's the first time ever that I ran someone over."

Aaron had a sip of his tea and shook his head.

"Henry, I lost it all. Lost all of my money."

"Ran over your legs, though, that's all. Slow and smooth, and it looks like it was pretty much painless."

"Nine thousand dollars, cash money. Oh my God."

Henry then added a squirt of extra Top Whip to Queenie's Jello. It was good Jello, firm and well cooled. She picked up a lime-green cube of it in her fingers, turned it this way and that, held it up to the light and examined the surface striations.

"The money was like a package, solid, wrapped in one of those fat elastic bands. I dropped it out there, somewhere."

"Had I driven, Aaron, I tell you, with less care or without the girls, I'd have flattened your head. We would not be having this conversation."

"I think I must have pulled it out by mistake. Got my gloves out of my pocket, that's when it must have happened. Fell out. I patted my pocket where the money was. Where's it gone? Fallen to the ground, that's the only place. Nothing but darkness. Down I went on my hands and my knees, the whole night long, four, five hours and the fog, what, an inch away? Not even that. A blind man, hopeless. Finally, I'm played out, I lie down. Bang, sometime later you run me over."

Aaron Stoodley was making no sense. He never had anything like that kind of money.

"A thousand dollars I'd give, as a reward, to get hold of that money again."

Talking to Aaron that morning was like squeezing the bottom of a tube of Pepsodent. There was toothpaste in there somewhere but it took a half hour to drag his story out in some kind of sequence.

It seems that about three weeks ago Aaron got a letter with two names he never heard of at the top corner. Lawyers in Halifax, it turned out. They wanted to give Mr. Aaron Stoodley nine thousand dollars because some relatives of his had died over there, on the mainland, and somehow the money they left had come down to him. These distant relations had all died from botulism, sadly—they were young—all at one go, their food full of poison and down they went, all in a terrible heap. He asked his grandmother, Priscilla, "We're related to these boys?" "Yes, yes it's terrible, death visited upon them so cruelly. Such young men. Cousins, what a shame."

Aaron drove all the way to St. John's, to the bank, as instructed, to see if it could possibly be true.

To his eternal wonderment and surprise, it was. He was handed the money by a lady in a suit. A real cheque with red numbers, but Aaron asked for it, "Please, please, in cash." "No problem, Mr. Stoodley, here you go," and she wrapped the dollar bills and snapped a big elastic band around them, cinching them at the waist.

He left the bank and walked down Water Street like a merchant prince.

Queenie switched to red-cube Jello for her second helping. She was quiet, always deep in thought for a girl her age, "still waters" as Eunice said. She wrinkled her forehead. She was never any trouble at all to take care of. Read her a book, sing her a song, she was happy.

She dipped her hand in and out of her purse and looked at Aaron Stoodley.

"Despite my riches, Henry," Aaron said, "I was still suffering, I was sore at heart. How'd you feel if your distant relatives up and died like that, so many, so young, and so all at once?"

"I wouldn't feel good about that," said Henry.

Aaron didn't spend a penny of his inheritance in St. John's. He came right back last night just as the fog came rolling in as thick as eiderdown, but damned if he didn't decide right then and there to walk one mile out of town. He was headed for Ed's Convenience Store, a sort of Shangri-La for Aaron Stoodley. The store had been for sale non-stop for seven years, and no way could he go by it without a turn of melancholy. He wanted to buy it. He wanted to buy it despite the fact that ten or maybe twenty cars a day went by. Once he tried to buy it on credit, on a promise.

"No money no way," is what Ed said to him, "you already owes me twenty dollars on red licorice. Some fool am I."

So now, when suddenly he had the funds, Aaron walked into the fog. A chill set in and he turned up his collar, pulled out his gloves, put them on, slapped his palms together in one of those surges of happiness and stepped out into the night. It was not until he'd gone twenty steps that he tapped his coat pocket, tapped it to feel the reassuring great chunk of money that was his. It was gone. The road-bed slanted hard into the ditch, the grass was thick, matted, invisible. For hours then, he crawled every inch of the path he'd taken, on his hands and knees, and he rolled gravel under his fingertips, raked through freezing puddles until pain and numbness were his constant companions and he cursed his own foolishness.

Then, as they all knew, Henry and the girls ran him over.

"I'd give a thousand dollars, Henry, to find it."

Wishful thinking, Henry thought, but understandable. Anything could disappear out there in the wilds and never be seen again.

Then Queenie reached into her purse and she pulled out a roll of paper money as big as her hand, maybe bigger, a big bank elastic on it tighter than a miser.

"Jeez Queenie, Jeez Queenie, Jeez Queenie, what the heck," was all Henry and Aaron said.

They sounded like two accordions tuning up.

Aaron was as good as his word, he gave the reward money to Queenie right there. He smacked his lips, peeled off a thousand dollars from the money roll and handed it back to her.

That's how Eunice and Henry and Queenie got their nest egg for the tar sands. They put it in the bank. That's how Aaron Stoodley went out and made an offer on the convenience store. That's how Eunice and Henry ended up owing their little girl, Pasquena, known as Queenie, one thousand dollars. They borrowed it from her.

"We'll pay you back when you're sixteen, or twenty-one," they said.

"Lucky we bought that purse," Henry said to Eunice later, when they were in bed, "instead of that cheap little locket."

She knew what he meant. At K-Mart, Eunice had wanted to buy the locket. Henry liked the purse. Queenie didn't care one way or the other but what did Henry know about girls, about presents? Anyway, they did buy the little purse.

"See, Eunice, I'm trying to figure out how Queenie could have jammed all that money of Aaron's into that little locket you wanted to buy."

They were curled up close together, Henry behind her.

"The one with the clasp, the little clasp that looked like it would break right off? Eunice?"

There was no answer. She was asleep.

Fact is, if they'd gone and bought the locket, they'd have been just as happy. They might have had a different story to tell though, and a little less money in the long run. And Aaron Stoodley wouldn't really have cared either. He'd gotten run over and lived to tell about it. How much greater than money was that?

tele-scope

FOR AT LEAST three months now, Hilda Cluett had stood to one side of her kitchen window and watched the teacher, Albert May, eat his dinner, either outside on the school steps when the weather was fine or, when it turned cold, she could see him with his feet up on his desk, and it was always the same: Cabot bread, peanut butter and jam, a thermos of tea—amazing, she thought, the detail she could see through the old telescope, though it had to be tipped this way and that when the reflection of the sky shimmered, totally amazing it was; sometimes, believe it or not, even through her lace curtains, she could read his watch for the time of day and see the rise and fall of his breathing, which often seemed synchronous to her own, and all of this, mind you, through this one small telescope—steady now—all brass, left to her thirteen years before when her husband, John Cluett, fell from the deck of his dragger into Halifax Harbour, weighed down by three sweaters, a woolen overcoat, oilskins, heavy boots, a mortgage of three thousand dollars, and a photo in his wallet of Hilda Cluett, then Hilda Hickey, age twenty-one, out at the barasway, squinting into what must have been a high sun, so unguarded she was.

the house-painters

"HE COULD PAINT houses."
"Clyde?"
"He could use the money."
"For sure."
"We could set him up."
"He'd need a ladder. Does Clyde go up ladders?"
"Not sure. I've seen him on a stepstool."
"Like in the kitchen?"
"That's it."
"How'd he look?"
"Fine. Steady. Mind you it's not that high."
"What else?"
"He'd need a hat with a brim."
"The brim, it keeps the paint off."
"That's right. Lots of times you look up."
"He'd need one of them flat chisels too, for peeling off the old paint."
"A scraper."
"That's it, start of every job. Scrape the old paint off."

"That's the hard part."

"Too hard, you ask me."

"The rollers for the walls, that's easy."

"Clyde could do rollers."

"Trouble is, you can't use the rollers on clapboard. It's a bad fit."

"That's the truth. For that you need a brush, the old kind."

"The kind with a hand-grip."

"So we sets him up with a ladder, a hat with a brim, a brush or two, and a chisel."

"He needs an outfit too."

"Like baggy pants?"

"Baggy pants, baggy shirt, hat with a brim."

"Keep the T-shirt clean."

"Clyde wears them shirts for days and days."

"*Save the Great Auk.*"

"I'm sick of that one."

"Me too. Worse shirt ever. I could care less about the Great Auk. It's a bird, isn't it?"

"It was. It's not anymore."

"You know that Clyde, there's a boy needs too much help. High maintenance, that's what he is."

"Them stories he writes? They're useless for money."

"I heard that. Never tried it myself."

"Don't, is my advice. You'd perish."

"Writers drink."

"Not Clyde."

"True enough. Rare you see Clyde with a drink."

"So the plan is, we set him up as a housepainter, we teach him how to do it."

"Sounds good. Good to help Clyde out."

"How much would he make?"

"Can't pay him by the hour, he's way too slow."

"You'd go under."

"For sure."

"Let's think about the best place to start."

"Shea Heights."

"Hamilton Avenue, I'd say."

"Why there?"

"Worn-out houses there, lots of them on the hill."

"Fine."

"This is how it works. You and I, we do the quote. Hamilton Avenue, any old house, there's one, we stop the truck, turn the wheels into the curb."

"Turn the wheels?"

"It's steep. That way, no runaway vehicles. It's happened."

"To you?"

"Once, and that's enough. Anyway, then we look up at the house like the experts we are."

"Supposed experts."

"No, real experts, that's how you pull it off. You stand back, you take a look. There, the back side of that house, on the east, that's the sunrise side, it's all peeled up. On the front side west, there's five layers of paint, one on top of the next. There's pink, then red, then blue, then white and then there's the oldest one of all. Yellow. Dig at it with the knife."

"Pocket-knife. I got one."

"That's fine, that's all you need. Then the windowsills. They're all messed up with the dry rot. You run your hand along there, splinters."

"That's no good."

"Then inside we go. Hi there Mrs. So-and-So, let's say Mrs. Ferris, open up the windows please, the old sash windows. Try again. They're stuck solid, fifty years. That don't make it easy. What about the fancy, fine work? Back outside again. There's the electric meter, you got to paint all around it, and the round window up there with the harbour view, you need a steady hand for that all right. The mailbox right by the front door, picture of a whale on it? It'd take an hour with a tiny brush to smooth around that. You need a wipecloth for the little drops. They're not cheap. Top it off, old Mrs. Ferris, she's got the front cement footstep painted kind of a dark red."

"For that, clean that off, you need chemicals."

"Damn right. The kicker though is the overhanging roof. Try to paint that. Three feet it hangs out. Up on the ladder, high up there, you got to lean back, way back."

"Add lots of money for that. Danger pay."

"Then we eyeball the square footage of the whole house, measure here and there with the tape, add it all up on a piece of lined paper."

"Clyde can't make a quote. His mind don't work that way."

"For sure. That's why we do it."

"So you and I, we set him up, we make the quotes, we drives Clyde to the job, we leaves him there till 5 p.m."

"How much for us?"

"Eighty percent for the backers, I say."

"Say the quote's two thousand dollars."

"That's way too cheap."

"That's how you get the job, that's how it works. Lowball. That'll be two thousand dollars, Mrs. Ferris, is what you say."

"You write it out?"

"Oh no, that's fatal. Verbal quote, a handshake, that's all."

"Discount for seniors, they all do that."

"Darn right. Widow discount too. Ten percent for each."

"She's a widow?"

"Most of them are."

"Then you sets Clyde to work."

"He scrapes off the front of the house."

"The up-high part?"

"That's why the ladder. Start up high I say."

"Then we come back, Clyde's still up there with the chisel, and we says, Mrs. Ferris, my dear, the dry rot on this one window frame is going to eat up the whole quote I gave you last week. We needs a re-figuring."

"Twelve thousand dollars."

"That's it. At least. Otherwise, I'm afraid, Mrs. Ferris, we're off to Mount Pearl with the crew."

"The crew?"

"Well, Clyde. Clyde's the crew. Not much of a crew, but he is the crew."

"There's no dry rot in Mount Pearl, Mrs. Ferris, all the houses there is brand new. All you needs in Mount Pearl, Mrs Ferris, is a roller and a tray. They don't have none of this old clapboard, they got vinyl. This old house costs a lot of money just for the up-keep."

"She might say, that's the trouble, living here in the old part of town."

"Then you says, Sorry to hear about the death of Mr. Ferris, Mrs. Ferris."

"It's been ten years, she says."

"Ten years, that's a long time."

"It's a long time but still she cries."

"Clyde'd be some mad, if he heard us talk like this."

"That's true."

"He's got a heart of gold."

"That's for sure."

"He knew she was a widow, he'd work for free."

"Clyde would do that. That's like Clyde."

"So we keep it secret. We say, Clyde, don't you go talk to this old lady. She lost her mind years back, she tells lies."

"She tells lies?"

"Not only does she tell lies, but she poisons food with rat poison."

THE HOUSEPAINTERS

"Rat poison?"

"Not only does she poison food with rat poison, she got fleas inside."

"Inside what?"

"Inside the house. She got ten cats."

"Why would you go tell Clyde that?"

"You know Clyde, say she invites him in, cup of tea. He'd go in, he'd listen, he'd get nothing done. It's for Clyde's own good, we keep him in the dark."

"You're right. Why the fleas?"

"Fleas is for sure when you got ten cats."

"Mathematics."

"That's right."

"First day then, we leave Clyde, we get back, what's he done?"

"He got the ground-floor windowsills scraped down. Perfect smooth. Nothing else."

"All day, two windowsills."

"That's why Clyde works by the job, not by the hour."

"That's it."

"First week on the job it's nothing but scraping down. Clyde and the paint chisel."

"Ladder training too."

"You ever seen a bucket of paint come down?"

"What do you mean, come down?"

"I mean a bucket of paint from the top of the ladder. It's sitting there and then Clyde makes the wrong move and there's a bucket of trim, purple trim, turning over and over in the air."

"I seen that once but it wasn't Clyde."

"The paint, the trim, you got to watch out."

"I can see that. Strong wind, the purple trim flies out of the can like it's caught in one of them pinwheels."

"Then it hits the ground."

"Boom."

"Mrs. Ferris then, you hope she's got one of them diseases of the eyes."

"Cataracts."

"That'll do. She wears them google glasses."

"That's it, that's what you hope."

"So out she steps from the door and she says, what was that bang I heard?"

"Oh that bang, dear? That's nothing, the truck door got took by the wind, is all."

"Meantime the paint's up to your knees and all over the side of the house."

"Sorry, Mrs. Ferris, sorry."

"Who says that? Me?"

"No, that's what we hear Clyde shouting, from up high. I can hear him now."

"And she'd say, sorry for what, young man?"

"That's when we'd say, real fast, we'd talk soft so Clyde couldn't hear, we'd say, the boy up on the ladder, Mrs. Ferris, he said he's sorry to see the condition of the roof."

"The roof? What's wrong with the roof?"

"It's got holes in it, for the water to get in, Mrs. Ferris. Storm damage from the ice and snow. Common thing here. Shame what it does. It needs fixing."

"My my, she might say, I don't know, I don't know."

"That's right, that's what she'd say."

"Hard to take bad news, you're that old."

"They get used to it."

"For another four thousand dollars, Mrs. Ferris, that's a roof we fix up watertight. Mr. Ferris, he's alive, he'd roll in his grave, he could see that leaky roof over your head. You being a widow. There there, don't snuffle. Clyde, you got one of them drip rags? Throw it down."

THE HOUSEPAINTERS

"Then in we go with the old lady, we ask for a glass of water."

"Thirsty? Us?"

"No no, up we go to the second floor, by the window where Clyde's at. We throw the water from the cup, up against the ceiling. Mrs. Ferris, Mrs. Ferris, look at this, we cry out. It's leaking wet."

"Four thousand dollars? Five thousand? she says, is there no end?"

"Cheap for the price, Ma'am, look, already the rain from last night is come creeping through the roof. Look at the floor now, there's a wet spot."

"She tries to look up but she gets dizzy."

"That's right. Those old necks, they can't look up."

"Arthritis, it pinches off the blood."

"That's sixteen thousand dollars now, she says, I don't know, I don't know."

"A lot of them old people, seniors, that's all they got. A few thousand."

"Now you sound like Clyde."

"How old's the roof, Mrs. Ferris? How many years you had that roof? She says, I thinks it's just three years old, the roof."

"Three years! Oh no! Clyde out there, the boy on the ladder? He says twenty years from the look of it, the roof. It's covered with green moss and there's holes in it."

"Clyde won't hear, he won't find out?"

"Not Clyde. His head's in the clouds."

"Hey wait a minute. We set Clyde up with the ladder, the hat and the outfit."

"Well?"

"Clyde can't do the roof."

"Clyde won't do the roof. Clyde paints. We do the roof."

"We never done a roof."

"Clyde's down there now at the bottom, he does the mailbox

with the tiny brush. He'd like that. The exact same time, we goes up the ladder, just the two of us, we bang on the roof with hammers for a bit, then down we come."

"That's it?"

"That's it."

"Mrs. Ferris, we says, there's your roof now. No leaks, guaranteed."

"The way you said that, that's not even a lie. There's your roof, you said. That's all."

"That's the truth all right."

"Eighty percent for us? Of the money?"

"That's right. At least."

"Then we go back in. Hey, smell that bad odour, Mrs. Ferris, that oil smell?"

"Oh my no, she says, not the furnace."

"Might just be a faulty burner, we seen that lots. The fuel oil puddles up."

"Oh my, she says."

"Trouble with the fuel oil when it puddles, Ma'am, it leads to fumes. Toxic fumes. Die in your sleep fumes. Maybe that's what happened to Mr. Ferris, when he woke up all dead? There there, my dear, the snuffles."

"Lucky thing, we know oil furnaces."

"Let's go down, we says to her, Mrs. Ferrris, we'll have a look. Oh my. Look at the puddling there. Smell them fumes."

"That you, Clyde? Stay out till you got the wall done and finished, we're fine down here."

"Powerful fumes, Mrs. Ferris, you could have a fire."

"You could die in your sleep, Mrs. Ferris, I promise you that, you got no sense of smell left over. Your nose is gone, the nerve endings in your nose."

"One spark, the whole downtown goes up, like 1892 all over again for the second time. Whoosh."

"We can fix that burner easy, got a spare in the truck. Thousand dollars is all."

"Oh my oh my, I do not know, she says."

"By the by, that's a real nice old chest of drawers you got here, Mrs Ferris. Shame you tuck it away down here, in the basement. Too damp, it should be up in the dry air."

"We could take that old chest up, get it checked out for value."

"Too heavy for the two of us. She's no help, she's useless for that."

"Go get Clyde. The three of us, we can squeeze this up the staircase."

"It did come down, didn't it? Has to go back up."

"That's right. Go get Clyde."

"I'll get him all right. Don't say nothing about the roof, the furnace or the floors."

"The floors?"

"The hardwood floors in the hall and the front room. You didn't see?"

"No."

"They're wore off right down to the wood."

"The shine's gone off?"

"Right off, down to the bare wood."

"That's bad. They won't last like that. Mrs. Ferris, you seen the state of your floors up there?"

"Oh wait. Here's Clyde to help. Hi there Clyde, give us a shoulder down here, we got to get this up the stairs."

"It's your old grandmother's chest of drawers, from down Boxey Harbour, that's what you say, Mrs. Ferris, two hundred years old? Should be worth some money for that. Eighty dollars, maybe more."

"Push harder Clyde. Trouble with you, kid, you got no muscles. Don't say a word to the old lady now, you know her nerves is bad."

"A thousand dollars, Mrs. Ferris? Who told you that? Oh no,

I don't think so, look at the age of the wood. Clyde, what you done? You snap that foot off, down goes the value on this piece of old furniture. Homemade it looks like. Then, we're upstairs, we say, thanks Clyde. Lift it up in the back of the truck. Then we say, Clyde, go back to work."

"That'll be eighty dollars now for the chest of drawers, Mrs. Ferris. Deposit. Sure, cash'll do. Oh you keeps a bit of handy money there by the stove? That's a smart thing, the banks, they're not open every day. Not Sunday. The eighty dollars you give to us is for the care of the chest of drawers. We give you back the same identical eighty dollars later, don't you fret. We know this man, down Water Street. He sells these things for a living. Oh that's a nice little writing desk you got there too. No no, don't cry, we'll leave the desk, Mrs. Ferris, you need that, to write things out. Cheques and letters. It's from the other side of the family, from old Mr. Ferris? Well, that looks like gold leaf on the leather, that's a fine desk. Not too often you see a desk like that, here on Hamilton Avenue these days. Maybe put it in the truck too, after all, save the money on the gas and we get it checked out too. Take that old photo off there, please Mrs. Ferris. That the kids? They look nice. All gone to the mainland, what a shame. Lonely times these."

"It's up on the truck now too, the desk. That was easy. You stay inside, Mrs. Ferris, we'll be back. Hey Clyde, you OK?"

"He's actually working pretty hard today."

"He says he likes Mrs. Ferris."

"He says he reminds her of someone."

"It sure isn't his sister, Meta Maud."

"No way. Why, she's some pretty, Meta Maud. Clyde lost out there on the looks. Seen Loveta recently, by the way?"

"I have and I count my lucky stars I have."

"Hey, you ever notice something? Like we talk a lot but we don't seem to think?"

"That's us, that's normal."
"I think I know why. Got a smoke?"
"There you go. Why?"
"Because Clyde is making all this up now."
"Our Clyde?"
"Our Clyde. Clyde Grandy."
"What do you mean, making it up?"
"I mean he wrote it all down, made it up in his head."
"That's not true. It was our idea."
"Set him up as a painter, that was our idea?"
"I think so, that was us. Sure it was."
"I think somewhere along the line, it became Clyde's."
"Maybe he heard what we said."
"To the old lady in there."
"We know he got big ears."
"He can hear a pin drop in Carbonear, that's what Meta Maud says."
"Oh no. If Clyde heard what we said to the old lady, he'd be mad."
"The roof, the floors, the furnace."
"Real mad. He'd think of some way to get us back."
"I didn't even mention the electric."
"He'd write things down I bet."
"He'd make things up."
"He does that."
"That's all he does, Clyde Grandy. Useless for everything else."
"But that's him up there now, on the ladder."
"He heard us, I know he heard us."
"Look at him up there. He's looking our way. Peering down."
"Twenty per cent of twelve thousand dollars, that's all for him. For us, five thousand each."
"He don't think that way."
"No."

"He is not financially motivated."

"Maybe go back into the kitchen, get some of that money from the lady's juice can? Before Clyde wises up?"

"He knows already. He's writing down what we say."

"Right now?"

"That's right. I'm pretty sure."

"He's putting these words in our mouths."

"That's right."

"We are the puppets of Clyde. Not the other way around."

"That's what I think now."

"Writers, they make things up."

"That's right, for the social good is what he said to me once."

"I don't think we're the social good."

"Well, we are for Clyde. Otherwise he wouldn't have a job."

"It was our idea to set him up."

"He had no money at all, no ideas to boot."

"We felt sorry for Clyde, now look."

"He's gone turned us into one of his stories."

"That's what I think. I'm not in charge anymore of the words that are coming out of my mouth."

"Me neither, I know what you mean."

"I think it all started with the desk."

"The one we put in the truck?"

"That's right."

"That's when Clyde took over?"

"I think so. Try saying something on your own."

"I don't think I can."

"I told you, we are the puppets of Clyde Grandy."

"What if someone finds out?"

"No way. Not from Clyde. He's got no talent, that's what I heard."

"He types a lot."

"That's true."

THE HOUSEPAINTERS

"He could be getting better."
"That's true."
"Better not take a chance is what I say."
"What've we done that's wrong?"
"Nothing, I don't think. Made her cry a bit."
"That's all we did. Made her cry."
"There's the eighty dollars cash. Deposit we said."
"That was for us, right?"
"It was but we're still here. Leaning on the truck."
"Not too late for us."
"The long arm of the law."
"What do you mean?"
"Fraud."
"That's what we did?"
"Almost."
"Let's give the money back to the old lady."
"Let's do that. Knock on the door."
"What about the stuff in the truck?"
"Take it off, give it back."
"What about the roof?"
"Forget the roof."
"The furnace, she'll think about the furnace."
"I don't think so. Her memory's gone."
"Die in the night, she'll think. That's what we said. Fumes."
"Should be in a home."
"That's right."
"I feel better now."
"So do I. Knock on the door. Watch out for the wet paint."
"Clyde's finished up."
"He's coming down the ladder."
"I think I'm myself again."
"Too bad we have to give back all the money."
"That's right. Well, eighty per cent of it."

"Tidy sum for us all right, you add it all up. We have to give it back? We earned it, sort of."

"Shut up, here comes Clyde. Hey Clyde, give us a hand with this desk, boy, it's going back."

"Floors are bad in there, aren't they Clyde. Wore out right down to the wood. Maybe the old lady, she's so nice, we buff 'em up free of charge?"

"Why not I say, eh Clyde?"

"She's a widow after all, these ten years."

"Don't say that, says Clyde, I think she'll cry again."

"My lips is sealed."

"Thanks for the help, Clyde."

After that, the time he saved the old lady, Clyde Grandy began to write more and more. It seemed now that words came naturally to him. All those plays he'd seen at the L.S.P.U.? They made a lot more sense to him now. Mind you, there was no money in it, in writing, none at all, so the housepainting, that was good too. The bosses he had were the best in St. John's, it turned out. They'd drop him off in the mornings, usually there on Hamilton Avenue, with the sun coming up, and they'd leave him there alone all day. If it rained, they'd swing by and pick him up. It couldn't be better for the mind, all the quiet time, the fresh air, the hat with the brim. "Hi there, Mrs. Ferris," he waved at her every day. He felt different, like he could breathe, like he'd been popped open like a new can of paint.

otto bond

OTTO BOND, EVEN though he'd been up late the night before, rose early on the morning of the championship game. The *twittering* of the birds woke him up. Twittering, that was the only word for it. They didn't call out or sing or moan like pigeons, they made their own little racket, but he didn't mind. The sun was shining and there was a nice breeze already coming up from the harbour, and the white curtains in the window, the common kind, the kind you could buy anywhere, swayed back and forth in such a pleasant way that he thought, *languorous*, that's it, that's the way those curtains move. They brushed back and forth on the windowsill and on the radiator and on the books he had piled there. Jeez, Otto Bond thought, this is the kind of day that everybody should be alive on, forever.

"Hey doggy-oh," he said to the little white dog who lay stretched out on the bed, "let's go."

Right away the dog jumped down onto the floor and Otto Bond opened up the door of the bedroom and the two of them walked out. Everybody else was eating breakfast already. Shawn Blagdon, the goaltender for the team, had his green soccer uniform on already because he was the type that had to get psyched up early. It was twelve hours before they blew the whistle and the game started.

"Hey there, Otto Bond," said Justin Peach.

"Hey," said Otto Bond. "I'll be back in a minute."

He got the dog leash down from beside the door and the others heard him whistling as he walked down the stairs, and the door closed. They lived across from a park.

"What time did he get in?" said Shawn Blagdon. "Three a.m.'s my guess."

"So much for the curfew," said Justin Peach.

"Bridie, the pizza girl, she's the problem," said Barry Rose.

"Give me that problem," said Johnny Drake.

Otto let the dog go from the leash and he got up on a park bench and balanced on one foot on the back.

"Gyroscopic," he said, and he spun around.

It was one of those solid benches they sank in concrete. That way, nobody could come by late at night, tip it over, throw it in the river, burn it up in a bonfire with liquor running through their crazy heads, out of control. He'd seen that done a few times, as an observer.

Then he jumped down and he and the little dog went back inside.

"Great day," he said.

"Three in the morning, Otto Bond," said Shawn Blagdon.

"All-Halifax," said Otto Bond, "that's us tonight, the champions, the best."

"We need you, that's for sure. You're the man," said Justin Peach.

"A recipe for disaster," said Shawn Blagdon, "you get whacked out by the pizza girl on the night before the game. Three a.m. That's why the curfew we made."

"Please pass the Special K," said Otto Bond.

He picked up a magazine that was there on the table, and as he ate he flipped through the pages. Then he laughed out loud.

"Listen to this you guys." he said, "In 1955, after the suspension of the superstar Maurice "The Rocket" Richard, fans in Montreal rioted and destroyed dozens of businesses along Ste. Catherine Street. A policeman who was injured in the riot said, *I don't know, they've all gone ape-shit.*"

Otto Bond laughed again.

"What's ape-shit?" he said.

No one knew, they'd never heard of that.

"It must mean wild, crazy, that sort of thing," said Justin Peach.

"I don't know," said Otto Bond, "I think it must mean wild, sure, but maybe wild and free, uncontrolled. Could even be happy. I like that, *ape-shit.*"

Two blocks away, Bridie had already changed the baby's diaper twice that morning.

"Oh my darling," she said to her baby who laid on his back, kicking his arms and legs, "what's up with all this mess? Eat something bad? Oh, that babysitter! I should have known. That's the last time for her, I promise you that."

It was her own mother who was the babysitter. There was no way that her own mother would slip up, not in a thousand years. All she had to do, which was all that Bridie had to do, was give Liam the bottle of formula after she heated it up.

"Hi there," Otto Bond said to Bridie, the first time they met.

He'd walked into the store and just leaned on the counter with both elbows. It was three weeks ago, early on in her shift, and there were no other customers there at all.

"Hi," Bridie said back to him.

He looked right at her. His eyes didn't shift away and he didn't jiggle from foot to foot.

"Pepperoni, if that's on the menu," he said.

Also, he smiled. There was nothing about that smile that made her feel uncertain. It was just there, his smile.

"Small, medium, or large?" she said.

She'd had a dream that, someday, someone like Otto Bond would walk into the shop, but it had never happened.

"Small pizza, that's for me, I like the small kind. The flavour stays better."

"It does?"

"Might be the small size of the box. Traps the aroma inside."

"I don't think so," she said.

She punched a few random numbers on the cash register so the drawer flew open. The internal bells rang cheerfully and then she pushed it closed.

"It's science," he said, "it's simple, the small box retains the heat and the molecules of cheese and pepperoni and crust that float around inside. There's less dissipation. No room for the flavours to vanish into the larger atmosphere."

"That's crazy. If everybody thought that, that's all we'd sell, the small ones. And the opposite is true."

Then she turned around to the back of the store and she raised her voice.

"Hey Jules, a small pepperoni."

"You got one of those out there already," said a voice from the back.

"We need a fresh one. This one's been here a while."

"Just heat it up."

The face of Jules then appeared in the opening from the back. He looked at Otto Bond.

"Since yesterday morning, Jules," she said.

"Heat it up, heat it up, it's fine. That's what the microwave is for."

And then Otto Bond said to Bridie, "That's okay, sure, just heat it up, I'm easy."

Bridie shrugged and heated up the day-old pizza and then she boxed it up and handed it over the counter.

"How tall are you, if I may ask a personal question?" said Otto Bond.

"Me? Five-two, plus these shoes."

"A small package too."

Bridie smiled.

"I get it," she said, "aren't you the clever one. There's not much you can do with these old pizzas, when they're not fresh. Sorry. It's Jules, that's the way it is around here."

"It's okay," he said. "I'll see you around, Bridie."

For once she was happy that she had the name tag on.

He walked out of the pizza shop and though she didn't have a clue, he was saying to himself enchanting, enchanted, how I love the name, Bridie.

The re-heated snack was no good though. He ate two bites of it before he threw into a trash basket down the street.

Two days later she was walking through the park. The sun was going down and she had the baby in the stroller. There was a bunch of boys playing soccer.

"Let's have a look, Liam, those are boys, they're playing soccer. You can do that someday."

She and the baby didn't get too far when suddenly the soccer ball bounced their way. One of the players broke away from the others and came over to get it. It was like fate, the way the soccer ball rolled right into the front of the stroller and stopped. The soccer player came over and stood there, but the sun was behind him and she couldn't see his face.

"Bridie," he said.

She shielded her eyes and she saw who it was.

"Oh, hi," she said.

She felt her legs go out from under her a bit, they wobbled at the knees.

"Fancy this," he said, "here you are."

"Hey Otto Bond, the ball!" said voices from the field.

That was the first time she ever heard his name. He turned away for a moment and with a real easy motion kicked the ball high in the sky. She had to block her eyes against the sun to see it rise in a black circle, get smaller and then fall in the distance.

"Who's this?" he said.

He nodded at the stroller.

"This is Liam," she said.

"Out with someone's baby? You're a babysitter too, as well as a pizza girl?"

He was smiling the same as he did in the store but he was covered with sweat this time.

"Oh, the baby's mine, this baby's mine."

"Oh Jeez," he said, "I never would have thought. Yours."

"We love the baby," she said.

Then she realized what she had said.

"Mother and me, we're the only ones. We love the baby."

"No father?" said Otto Bond. "For Liam?"

"He got run over by a train," she said.

That was a lie she told to everybody. It was automatic to her, by now. Sometimes she told that lie so often that she came to believe it, and she came to believe that she was the driver of the train, with her hand on the throttle full-blast.

"Jeez, that's too bad."

"It's okay. We got a nice life going on, for us."

"I can see that. My name's Otto Bond."

He held out his hand to her. She shook his hand and held onto it without any effort at all.

"I know," she said, "they're calling you. You better go, Otto Bond."

Those were the words she said, but it was the last thing she meant. He could have stood there till the sun went down, the world flipped over and China appeared in the sky. She was still holding his hand so she let go.

"That was a great piece of pizza you gave me. Never had better, at least the re-heated kind," he said.

So now they both told lies.

"That Jules, he's a bit of a loser," she said.

"I'll come back for more," he said.

He bent down and rubbed the top of the baby's head for a second. Then he turned and ran back to the field where there was a large circle of players all dressed the same, kicking balls around, bouncing them on the knees, hitting them on their foreheads. Soccer, that was their game.

All their jerseys said *Falcons*. Obviously, they were a team.

That's how their relationship started, with a piece of pepperoni pizza and a couple of small lies. That's why Bridie lined up for a ticket outside the stadium on the night of the championship game.

"No strollers in the stands," the guard said to her. "Leave it here."

She picked up the baby in the shawl.

The guard said to her then, "Don't worry, Miss, we'll have it here. Pick it up at the end of the game, I'll keep my eye out for you."

There were thousands of fans and by the time the game started, the stands were full and the lights were on as bright as could be, the sky dark above, and there was Otto Bond front and centre in his green uniform.

Shawn Blagdon had black gloves on, the ones he always wore, but he looked a bit nervous. He'd been throwing up in the locker room for the last half hour.

"Gentlemen," said the referee.

"You guys are a long way from home, just to lose," said the captain of the Raiders to Otto Bond.

"Well," said Otto Bond, "home's where the heart is, buddy,

and this is where we are tonight. Good luck to you."

The captain of the Raiders stood over him by at least a foot.

They shook hands and the game was on and for the first while, it didn't look too good. The evil Raiders came down into the Falcons' end of the field and they stayed there for ten minutes and if it hadn't been for Shawn Blagdon, the game could have been lost right off the bat. Four times, he flew through the air and deflected shots over the top of the crossbar. It was like a dream for him, like he'd seen all the shots before and he knew where to go before the kick was even made. The hometown fans groaned with disappointment as the Raiders missed one chance, then another. At the same time though, those fans were laughing. It looked like a cakewalk to them, if this kept up. It was just a matter of time. They were the Raiders, undefeated all year, heavy favourites to walk off with the trophy. Bridie knew nothing about soccer but she could see that her team, the Falcons, were back on their heels.

She held onto her baby while the stadium rocked around her and she said to him, "Oh my, Liam, this does not look good."

Then all of a sudden Johnny Drake lifted a long curling pass down through midfield where Otto Bond picked it off the top of the grass at full speed. He made about three quick moves with his head and his feet and then he exploded the other way and he danced past the last two Raiders. They looked foolish, those defenders, like they were little boys. The crowd sucked in their breath. There was Otto Bond with just the goaltender now in the way and Otto Bond leaned one way, the ball fired straight the other, and it was 1-0 for the boys so far from home. For the Falcons.

Bridie jumped up and down but she was the only one in the whole crowd, anywhere near her, who was happy. She held onto the baby needless to say.

"Look at that!" she said.

All the Falcons piled onto Otto Bond and then he looked up at Bridie in the stands.

"Yes," he said to himself.

He waved to her.

"There, see?" Bridie said to Liam, "he sees us."

She waved her hand and the baby's hand too.

"Sit down, sit down," someone said to her, "get out of the way."

She sat down the rest of the time till the game was half-over and it was half-time, a break in the action, still 1-0 for her team, for Otto Bond's.

"This can't be happening," all the fans around her said.

"Hey," Bridie said, turning to them, "this is happening! Look at the score!"

They all laughed and they said, "You wait, there's lots of time left for the slaughter. Want a beer, darling?"

"No," she said, "I'm the designated driver."

She showed them the baby and they laughed.

"You breastfeeding?" they said.

"That's none of your business."

"Go right ahead, you want to, we're not shy."

"Let the baby drive home," someone said.

"Maybe I will," said Bridie.

Someone gave her an open beer and she drank it. Soccer was okay, her first game ever. She could do this lots of times.

Then the second half started and those damn Raiders came on strong again and even though Shawn Blagdon dove to the left and to the right, and even though Otto Bond struck here and there like lightning, now the Raiders were all over him like glue, two or three players at a time. The writing was on the wall. In the fiftieth minute, the Raiders finally broke through with a low shot to the corner and the crowd went wild.

Now it was 1-1.

Shawn Blagdon hung his head. He hadn't seen that one coming.

But the other Falcons patted him on the back and Bridie could tell they were saying, don't worry, don't worry.

Five minutes to go in the championship game.

"There you go, sweetheart," the crowd said to her, "welcome to the real world. Prepare to lose."

Half of them were howling with the pleasure of it. More beer was passed around. "One for the baby?" they said.

"Okay," Bridie said, "but I better drink it for him. He's underage."

"Drink it fast," they said, "there's not much time left."

"Oh no, what now?" Bridie said to the baby, under her breath, into the baby's ear.

She had one arm around Liam and the other hand was on the beer she'd been given. Then someone shook up another beer bottle and sprayed it in the air and all the spray came down over her head and on the baby's head in a fine mist. She wiped off the baby's face with the side of her cheek. Liam never cried at all.

Then she said, "Hey! None of that! Watch out for the baby!"

"Sorry," they said, laughing some more, and they turned and sprayed the other way.

Then the crowd rose to their feet because here came the Raiders again. They moved the ball down into the Falcons' end. But they made a mistake. Justin Peach intercepted a pass. As soon as Justin Peach touched the ball, Bridie saw Otto Bond take off on the far side of the field. He was like one of those rockets that go into the sky on Victoria Day, even though he was still on the ground. Justin Peach was under pressure but he kicked the soccer ball over to Johnny Drake and then there it was, for the second time that day, the long arching pass with the tailwind, and Otto Bond was way downfield running it down. This time, determined, he shook off the three Raiders that were hounding him like they were gnats or bugs. He was knocked down in front of the net but he got up fast and with his right leg, he released the ball, and then fell backward to the grass.

That was it. The ball curved up and under the crossbar and the net bulged out. The goaltender lay on the ground like he was dead. Silence in the air. The referee waved his arms and he blew his whistle. The game was over. Bridie jumped back up to her feet.

"Get out of the view!" someone said.

"The view's over," she said. "Can't you see that?"

She ran down the steps of the stadium with the baby in her arms and she ran across the track and out onto the field.

Be careful, she said to herself, you've had those two beers. She slowed a little. The baby was wrapped up tight in the shawl across her chest, safe as can be. Otto Bond saw her coming and he came over to her and even though the baby was in the way, she leaned up to him and she gave him a kiss. Beer does that, she figured but she didn't care. He was covered with dirt and sweat.

"Hey watch out," said Otto Bond, "you'll squish the baby, he'll smother."

He put his arms around her and they circled in a little dance.

"I don't think so," said Bridie. "His head's free."

"Well okay, I can see that now," said Otto Bond.

He leaned back into Bridie and gave her a kiss, a longer one. If he tasted the beer from her lips, he didn't say anything.

"I'll take you home, give me a minute," he said.

Then he ran over and joined the other boys who were celebrating. All the Raiders had walked off and the Falcons had the field to themselves. Otto Bond took off his shirt and swung it around his head like a pinwheel and he ran in circles and he did a flip and he landed on his feet.

"Look," said Shawn Blagdon to the others, "Otto's gone ape-shit."

While the Falcons danced around in the centre of the field, Bridie and the baby stood off to the side and watched. She felt a bit dizzy from the excitement. She was sure it wasn't the beer. Three of the fans who'd been sitting near came up to her, all at different times.

"You need a ride home, honey?"

"No, I'm fixed up here. I got a ride thanks."

Then the security man came over with the stroller.

"You okay? You need a lift anywhere, I got a car."

"No, no I'm okay," she said, "thanks."

Otto Bond took her home. He didn't have a car so they took the bus and they got off at a stop near her place and he walked her the rest of the way. He was still in his soccer outfit. People looked at him but it wasn't that unusual, on the bus or on the street, in Halifax, to see someone dressed like that, in a soccer uniform.

"Thanks," she said, when they got to her place, "I had a great time and so did the baby."

"Seeing you there, that was the best, Bridie, that made it the best for me. It wasn't the goals at all."

"You mean that?"

"Cross my heart," he said.

She believed him, as she should have believed him because he was telling the truth.

He left her there and he walked the rest of the way home, to his own place, where the others were already waiting. What a day it was, what a night. He had nothing to complain about. He was high in the air. As soon as he got home, without changing his clothes, he took the little dog out for a walk.

"I'll be back," he said to the others.

He went to the playground in the park, to the far end. He reached up for the monkey bars. As the dog ran around in circles beneath him, barking, even though it was pitch black, Otto Bond swung there. He swung back and forth, and he swung higher and higher like he was a child again, maybe even like an orangutan would do, or a chimpanzee far off in the jungle of Sumatra. Or someone gone ape-shit.

Then he flipped through the air in a somersault and came down feet together in the sand. He stretched his arms upwards into the Halifax night.

He called the dog and felt the leash pull against his hand.

"Bridie," he whispered to himself.

Then they went back to the party, to the pizza party, to Justin Peach, to his homemade sauce.

sculpin

IT WAS A common thing to do on those long mid-summer days, when the sun was up for sixteen hours, when idleness brought them to the wharf with their bamboo rods and their lines of string: they hauled up sculpin after sculpin, sickly green and spiny "like a parboiled goat's head," said Thomas Keeping; they held the sculpin's jaws shut tight with finger and thumb, and with a small flat stick, they rubbed the smooth belly, gently, until the fish began to swell like a party balloon, a victim of its own internal gases, trapped by what they called devilment; then sculpin after sculpin would be thrown high into the air, down onto the ebbing tide with a flat smack, to float head-down and belly-up in a flurry of small rocks, flesh exploding on impact, or, if spared by some mathematical chance, out the sculpin would float, clumped together by wind and current until the gulls came, their beaks made for ripping and pulling, or until the young fishermen saw, from the wharf, the distant slow black flap of the eagle, from the cliffs at Farmer's Cove, stretching out his talons as he, too, passed the summer days in his own way, a predator on idle, with plenty of time to whet, to kill.

rick-shaw

THEY WALKED THROUGH the front door of the coffee shop. There was a bit of a line-up so they joined it, and they watched the women in their uniforms moving around behind the counter. When they finally got their coffee, they walked over to an empty table near the window, and they sat down.

"I got it, we set him up. A rickshaw."

"A rickshaw?"

"One of those Chinese taxis."

"You mean one of those carts, people in the back, someone pulling like a horse?"

"That's it. Fill it full of tourists, charge money."

"You seen that?"

"Victoria B.C. Big money maker out there."

"Clyde? You think Clyde Grandy could pull a rickshaw?"

"Sure. See the sights, trot along the harbour. Talk it up, Clyde would, he'd say, you see up there? That's Signal Hill, here's the boats from far away, here's where they used to pull in the fish. When there was fish. Then he'd catch his breath, then clippety-clop, Duckworth Street end to end."

There was something nice about the morning coffee ritual. Every day, they could let their minds go blank or, like today, they could let their dreams spin off into the air like pinwheels.

"Clyde pulls the rickshaw and he talks at the same time?"

"That's it. That's the only way. Tourists expect that, the palaver."

"Sounds like hard work."

"Well, that's true. It is hard work. That's how you do it though. I saw them out there, Victoria B.C."

"Hard work, pull and talk at the same time."

"For sure. No kidding. You learn to breathe easy, through the nose. That's my guess. That way there's no huffing or puffing."

"Horses breathe through their nose."

"Of course they do."

"Looks bad, huffing and puffing."

"I'll say. Customers wouldn't go for that, they'd feel bad."

"Clients you mean."

"Customers, clients, call them what you like."

"On the other hand, maybe they'd tip more, the worse you look. Horses, they froth and sweat. Clyde, there's no way he'd do that. Froth at the mouth."

"No, that's true. He'd pace himself. He's smart that way."

"How much, I wonder, you could charge for the rickshaw ride?"

Now and then they'd get talking so fast, there was barely time for them to think. Their coffee sometimes just sat there and got lukewarm and they had to go back to the counter, spill out a bit and top up.

"Downtown? Charge twenty dollars bare minimum. Couldn't do it for less."

"That's not bad money. Half an hour for that?"

"Imagine the upkeep on the horse. Feedbags. Twenty minutes, the harbour run. Charge more for the hill. Thirty, forty dollars for that, depending on the load."

"The hill? Signal Hill? No way, no one could get one of those rickshaws up there."

"You don't think?"

"He's got no muscles. You seen him with that shirt off?"

"Thin. Weasel-thin."

"He's skin and bone for the most part."

"Sinewy though."

"Secret wells of strength, sometimes, with sinewy."

"How high up, you figure, would Clyde have to go? If he could, say."

"The very top, for forty dollars. He'd have to go all the way."

"All the way up for the view, the breathtaking view."

"That's what they calls it. No tourist would be satisfied with less. There'd be hell to pay, if he only got partway up."

"Not sure why they call it breathtaking."

"Me neither. Every day it's the same up there, more or less."

The coffee shop was bordered on one side by a firehall, and on the other side by a row of houses made of wood. You could have been anywhere in the whole country, if you didn't look too far around. There was no obvious view of the ocean or the harbour, but there was a gull walking in the parking lot, stalking about like a courtesan. The gull looked real well fed, cocky, with a yellow beak and glinty eyes. He was there half the time, and half the time he was somewhere else.

"Cold up there at the top."

"Real cold. All you see is the ocean."

"Unless there's fog. Then there's nothing."

"Half the time it rains."

"But they don't know that, the tourists down in the harbour with the maps and the kids all crying, they don't know it's cold up there, do they?"

"No. That's right. They'd jump right in the rickshaw."

"Happy as clams."

"Clyde pulls the rickshaw straight up the hill."

"With his sinewy strength, his untapped wells of power."

"Forty dollars, thank you, ma'am, sir."

"More tips too, he talks the whole way."

"No way Clyde could do that. One or the other, not both. It's a long way up."

"I walked it once. Well, half-way."

For a minute, the two of them didn't say anything. They looked out the window of the coffee shop, and you could see that in their distant gaze, they were imagining Clyde Grandy. They were thinking about the skinny body he had, how he usually didn't talk a lot even when he wasn't pulling a rickshaw. With their coffee spoons, they idly stirred in more sugar, pouring it liberally from the container. It was getting warm. They loosened their scarfs and opened up the top buttons of their coats. Some of the wet dirt from their boots was now smeared on the tile floor, but that was expected. A boy with a mop and a bucket came around every hour or two.

"I wonder, rickshaws, they have brakes?"

"You just hold on to the bar. Real tight."

"You don't let go."

"That's it, that's the braking system. All models the same, last time I looked."

"Then Clyde'd need insurance, right?"

"Insurance? There you go, I hadn't thought of that."

"Me neither. Till now."

"My guess is, though, that insurance is not real cheap. Knowing those bastards."

"Ups the cost for the businessman."

"Bloodsuckers, parasites."

"What if Clyde's up there, and those little muscles of his give out? His sinews snap."

"Oh my oh my, spare me that."

"Down comes the rickshaw from the the hill."

"Trouble for the customers."

"Real trouble."

"Full speed, I can see it, the rickshaw in the air from the cliff, or down the road backwards, hits the rail by the water and up she goes high, high in the air."

"Trouble for Clyde."

"Trouble for us, we're the backers."

"That's why insurance."

"I got it. We put life jackets on the passengers, first off, then if they end up in the water, they float. They can be seen, they can be rescued."

"You mean, before they get in the rickshaw, we make them put on life jackets?"

"That's right."

"How'd they feel about that, I wonder."

"Not too good. That's my guess, but tourists like that sort of thing. Adventure travel. I read about it."

"I got it. Make the rickshaw look like a dory. Natural then, life jackets."

"Now there's a good idea."

"Jack up the price, we do that. Fifty dollars."

"You'd have to. All the kit, everything they'd need for the harbour crash."

One thing about the coffee shop was that sometimes there'd be a long line-up, like when they came in, and then, for no reason, there'd be a lull. That was the time to head back up for seconds. The two friends spotted their chance and jumped up and then they came back and sat down. By then, they had their coats off, draped over the chairs, so they didn't lose their place. Mornings, they nearly owned that table.

"Bad for business, crashes."

"Clyde, you know, I just don't know about Clyde."

"He did okay after all, the housepainting."

The shop was filled up with old retired men, those who had nothing to do. Most of the men had wives at home, the two of them guessed. Wives, girlfriends, why that'd be nice. It wasn't always best to be single. Both of them had been through lonely times themselves, hard private times recently, but it was the very last thing they'd ever talk about, their own troubles.

"He still write those stories?"

"Little ones."

"That's what he does?"

"That's what I heard, they're not real books. He doesn't have the staying power, I heard, for real long books. Right now anyway."

"There's money in that?"

"Clyde's never got a penny."

"That's not his thing, money."

"I've seen that. He's a scrounger."

"He reads all the time."

"Clyde's hopeless, that's the truth."

"Well, that's why we're here now, to try and figure out something more for Clyde."

"We are?"

"Well, that's one reason. The other's for coffee."

"Rickshaws, now, getting back to those, they're a scarce commodity, I'd say."

"Well, you're right there."

"How many you seen, lifetime?"

"Three, four."

"That's what I mean, they're scarce."

"Well then, I say this: let's not get our hopes up on rickshaws for Clyde."

"You mean let's be more practical?"

"That's right. Hard-nosed. Work on something else."

Now and then the double door to the bakery in the back opened. Then a wave of doughnut vapour and cookie and sugar wafted over them. They could almost drink it in, it was so thick. It made everybody there feel good.

"Practical. Well, forget rickshaws then."

"You know, I don't really care about Clyde. I don't see why you care so much about Clyde, that's all you talk about. Clyde, Clyde, Clyde."

"I don't care about Clyde. But I do care about someone else."

"Oh?"

"Meta Maud."

"His sister? His twin sister?"

"I can't help it. She's the one for me."

"That may be, but you're not the one for her, the last time I looked."

"The other day, she smiled at me. Never have I seen such beauty."

"Oh for the love of God."

"She is the prettiest girl this island has ever seen."

"Smart too, you're going to say."

"Everybody knows that."

"A lot better looking than Clyde."

"So's a Pekinese dog, better looking than Clyde."

"Funny thing, the two of them, Meta Maud and Clyde, twins and all. You figure it out."

"Meta Maud, she's got the jump, the brains, the looks. She's the package. I don't know what happened to Clyde. The other day, what'd she say to me? She said I was the very best. Those were the words she uttered, guaranteed. You are the best, that's what she said. First though she said, you can stop the banging now."

"The banging? What are trying to tell me?"

"The exact words. Meta Maud Grandy."

"She said to you, stop the banging? You and Meta Maud? Banging?"

"Well no, just me. She said, stop the banging in the pipes, in the radiator. So right off I bled the air off in a cup and the banging stopped, and then she said, you are the best. Also she said, find some more work for Clyde, please you got contacts."

"You have contacts?"

"Well, sort of. There's you."

Clyde Grandy had just walked up Long's Hill and, for a breather, he stopped and looked through the window of the coffeeshop at the top. At first, he couldn't see much because of the reflection of the sky in the plate glass. Then, just inside, two feet away, there were the two friends his sister had. The ones who set him up, housepainting. They waved at him. It wasn't the kind of wave that said come on inside and join us, Clyde. It was just hello. They sat there, those two, over coffee like they had nothing to do.

What kind of life was that? All they ever did was hash over this and that, non-stop. And they were all over Meta Maud too, whenever they saw her, like she was made of honey or molasses.

Clyde Grandy cupped his hands around his eyes and got even closer to the window.

Go ahead, look like a fool, he said to himself.

Madeleine. It tripped off his tongue, the name did, but she wasn't there, she wasn't out front serving. She must be in the back. The big doughnut machine would be humming away, and she'd have the hairnet on, with the trickles of sweat, the see-through gloves.

"What's Clyde doing out there?"

"Spying, it looks like."

"Casing the place?"

"The usual nothing is my guess."

Then the doors to the back, to where they made the doughnuts, swung open and out came Maddy into the store, with a tray piled high with honey-dips. Clyde's chest went thump like a kick and he jumped back from the window.

"Jeez, look at him hop."

"Stung by a bee?"

"Buckled his knees, whatever it was."

"Look at him out there."

"That boy needs something in his life."

"Tell me. Loose ends, that's him."

Madeleine bent down, and put the tray where it should be, and then she stood up and looked around. She saw the usual types, but hey, there's that boy again outside. The good-looking one with the scruffy jacket. She was getting sick of the others with the cars and the clothes, the Mall, the way they bellowed out down there on George Street, drunk by ten.

"I need a quick break," she said to the boss.

"Okay, Maddy."

That was the way he was, the boss, he was kind enough. She didn't even take the apron off when out she went into the street, but she did peel off the hairnet.

Inside the store, the two friends tried to read her lips, what she said to Clyde Grandy. Oh how they tried, but they were not trained in that skill, so it was hopeless. Who knows what it was. The two of them talked for five minutes out there, and they both laughed a bit together at the end, and Maddy twirled strands of loose hair, blonde, with her fingertip.

"Oh, Meta Maud, Meta Maud," the two friends said later to Clyde's sister, "you'll never guess."

"Never guess what?"

"The doughnut girl, Maddy, she spoke to your brother."

"She did? Well, maybe that's just what he needs, he needs someone like that."

"True, true," the two of them said, "that's what Clyde needs all right. That's what Clyde needs. A girlfriend. Someone with sense."

Then they left Meta Maud's house and stepped out together

into what was, by then, a darkening sky. Maybe it was even going to snow. They didn't talk at all down Military Road. At last they seemed lost for words. They walked towards home. They kicked leaves. And what did they think of? That's not too hard to guess. They must have thought, in secret to themselves: would it ever happen to me? Would someone like the doughnut girl ever talk to me? Surely it's my time, they would have said. Curl your finger in my hair, strap me into a rickshaw, I don't care how dangerous it is, take the brakes off, cast me into the harbour deep. Pull me out of deep water, lay me down at the bottom of that big high hill with all the love you got. Rescue me, rescue me from all this, this life of mine.

That's what the two of them would have thought, almost for sure.

Everybody thinks that way, one time or another.

the alchemists

IF I WERE rain, I'd gather over the harbour and look across the water at this our room and darken its windows slowly as in an overture, and then I'd scatter down obliquely and blur the outlines of the crumpled sheets and smother the sound of the phonograph spinning in the corner; I'd pour down in such a rush of testament force as to gut out candlelight and wash away the trace of everything we did, for deceit was then our sinuous way, forgetfulness befriended us, subterfuge inhabited every gesture, no touch or smile was pure, dark light passed through us as bent as in a prism, and no one knew that we were alchemists, that we'd been granted more than our share of time taken from that same rain now called upon, imaginary, sheets of it stinging down on days and nights when everything we did was wrong.

how it was for them

WHEN SHE LOOKED back at the wedding, which happened thirty-seven years ago, Rowena remembered that it was mostly okay. For one thing, no one said anything mean to her, and Jimmy was kind the whole time. He wasn't always like that, he could have got that glazed look on his face, moody. Even better, no one there saw that she was three months along, despite the fact that she was skinny as a rabbit. She had to work some to pull on that white dress. Then her mother said to her, "Don't stand sideways. Say hello straight on, that's the trick." Rowena stood by the window and looked out at the hills, at the snow. The snow had fallen overnight and it looked soft, wet and heavy, like it would melt.

For their first anniversary, it was a ring that he gave to her. She remembered how they were at the restaurant down by the harbour. He reached into his pocket and took it out, a little gold circle with a diamond. There it was.

"Hey," he said, "what's this, look at this."

There was no box around it, he had it held in his fingertips.

"Oh thanks," she said, "thanks, sweetheart, but this is way too much for me."

"No no," he said, "this is for you, you're the best."

"But the first one's paper," she said, "the first anniversary, like you get a card, a party hat, that's all, nothing like this. Then, the second year it's straw, then leather."

"Paper?" he said, "That's for them with no money. Hold it by the light, it's real. Real diamonds. Take it in and check."

Then they finished off the berry crumble.

Next year, he turned off the TV.

"Time for us," he said, "time for us."

So, up the hill where they lived, she put the baby to bed. Laid her down like a chalice and backed up tippy-toe. Colic. That'd be the last straw if she woke up now, twisted her little face and cried. It was all nerve wracking for her, nothing seemed simple. Maybe it wasn't colic, maybe it was something worse.

The third year, they liked to dance, so it was natural to go with the leather pants they both got on Water Street. Those pants shone better under the lights, black ones, they rubbed like skin. Quite a problem in the ladies' though, they turned out, what with all the tight peeling off and peeling down and the zipper that jammed up or down or, even worse, half-way one way or the other, going nowhere. That's why they make blue jeans, they figured one night, when they got home laughing. It was better now, their life together, it was going in the opposite direction of most.

For their fourth year, he brought flowers home from the high meadow. Nothing special, they were low and white with shiny green leaves, and all he did was put them in a glass of water on the table. The flowers were so small, they had no real stems, they floated around in the glass like they were on the move. There was a smudge on the glass, little whorls, so she wiped them off like a criminal would do, if there was a crime of any kind, and moved them dead-centre.

The next year, he was out cutting wood when she heard a thump, and then he came through the kitchen door. He held one hand in the other hand and there was blood under the handkerchief.

"Damn," he said.

"Quick, Jimmy," she said, "let me see that, sit down. There's a sharp piece of wood there, sticking right in."

"Take it out," he said.

She ran and got the pliers and grabbed the piece of wood and pulled it out, so fast her fingers got slippery with blood. It was an inch long, the piece of wood.

"Thanks, darling," he said, "you're the best."

She washed off her hands in the sink.

"You're my sliver girl," he said, "that's what you are."

Year six: she tucked the shirtsleeves over the pointed part of the board, and moved the iron around and around, and when she started out doing that, she watched the soaps on TV. Scorches? Those were the little areas of brown that showed up at the sad parts, there wasn't much you could do about that.

"Use the sprayer," her sister said, "use it more than that, cool it off. Touch the iron like that, wet your fingers, they won't burn if you're real fast."

So she did that and she got a lot better with the iron.

"Where'd the scorches go?" they all said.

She sprayed Maddy too when she got home, even on the cold foggy days. It got to be part of the games they played, six years in.

Year seven wasn't so nice. He came home at 3 a.m.

"Jimmy," she said, "I know she was there, you can't pull the wool over my eyes. Get out and go with your party girl."

She stood in the kitchen with one hand on the counter and then Maddy was there with bug eyes. He put his hand on her arm and looked guilty. There wasn't a lot she had to do. Without the two of them, he'd flip right out, she had him there.

"Get out, go," she said, but instead of that, he sat down in the armchair like the sag of misery he was, and he drummed his fingers up and down.

"Nothing happened," he said.

She didn't want this in her life, no way, so she put the hammer down. Lucky thing was, that was it.

For the eighth anniversary, he went out and got the baby boots bronzed.

"How'd you think of that?" she said.

"Eight years, it's bronze," he said, "so I figured, try the trophy store."

He was right. The window there was half-full of baby shoes that looked like caramel now, butterscotch with dust all over.

The guy in the store said, "The ones in the window, they're half-price, nobody showed up for them."

"But those are not mine," he said, "those are not Maddy's shoes."

"Well, the wife, she'll never know that," the man said, "it saves us both time and money, take two pair, I don't care."

"Two pair?"

"Sure go ahead. By the by, this here's a good business if you like."

"Good business?"

"Real good. Makes money, makes people happy. Trophies, bronze boots, what's better than that?"

He was the only customer in the store so all he did was order Maddy's boots, bronzed, and when he came back to get them, he also bought an old trophy for himself that said First Place, Husbands.

On their ninth anniversary, they went shopping.

"There's always something nice about pottery," she said, "look at the glazes." They were at the east end of Duckworth Street. All he could smell was flowery soap and beeswax and the lavender, if that's what it was, in the little bags. There were small price tags on everything.

"You like the teapot?" he said.

"That's the one, I like the glaze on that one, not so shiny."

"Eighty-five dollars," he said, "that's a lot of money for a teapot."

"It's the only one like it," she said, "it'd be ours, only forty dollars each, really." Well, that made sense to him, that's not a bad deal at all.

"Done," he said.

He picked it up and put his fingers through the handle. It had real good balance, it wouldn't be easy to drop that one on the floor into twenty pieces, scattered through the kitchen like a bomb went off.

Tin ceiling? Sure, look at that. There was a time all the stores were like that downtown, before the fires and the codes and the dropped ceilings low enough to make you sick, but that's beside the point.

"You could have an art gallery here," he said, "Rowena, some kind of store for selling. Paint all you like in the back, wear your smock, have a foghorn or a bell on the door. Why not? Here's where the tourists go by, that's where they get on the bus for the Hill."

"But it's a restaurant," she said.

"With food like this," he said, "it's not going to be a restaurant for long. This place is going under, you can feel it."

He was right, the waitress was lost in some kind of conversation on the phone in the corner.

"She crying? I hope not," he said, "you got to learn to keep yourself together at work."

They ordered food from the kitchen. You could see the cook was bored, he looked out through the porthole. They ate the fish, the vegetables. It was their tenth anniversary, the baby-sitter with the Russian name, Sonja, the one with an accent, was back home with Madeleine, so there was no worry there.

He noticed the ad in the Telegram under Vintage Cars. He dialed up the number and the guy said, "Come on over, you're the third one."

"It's a Studebaker Silver Hawk?" he asked.

"It's a Silver Hawk, like brand new."

When he got there, all he could think was, wow, that's a lot of steel, turquoise like turquoise colour can only be on cars like that, better than in real life, and the grill had the highest shine. Not a fingerprint anywhere. He opened up the hood and he backed off and he saw his father looking in.

"How much is this?"

"Eight thousand dollars, no more no less and there's others coming."

"Sold," he said, "that's for my wife on our anniversary."

"Oh, the wife likes cars, vintage cars?"

"Not yet," he said, "but she's going to like this one the moment she sets her eyes on it, guaranteed."

Then they took four years off. There were no presents at all, the budget was blown sky high and it wasn't easy to forget. The Studebaker filled the whole garage, and the bicycles and the lawn-mower and the ladders all got stacked outside in the rain till he put up the wooden shed he bought from the tire store. She never took to that big car at all.

"Look, it's the colour of your eyes," he said.

She never drove it, not once.

"Look at your face in the grill," he said, "how pretty you look in that grill."

What nonsense that was, her face was swelled and distorted and bent in and out like a side-show mirror.

"Don't scratch the car for God's sake," he said, "watch your buttons, when you go by."

So they passed the silk year, the lace year, the ivory year, one by one unrecognized but for the turquoise-blue monster Studebaker that they took out on Sundays. What'd they do? They drove it as far as Butter Pot and she had to admit, there was lots of room in that car for a picnic basket. There was even more room when Maddy quit coming. She liked her friends better, she wore blue eye shadow all the time.

For their fifteenth anniversary, they lay awake and waited for the phone to ring. Maddy was real good about that, about phoning.

"Mommy, I'm staying over at Ally's, we're doing homework."

"Okay honey, that's good, can I speak to Ally's mother?"

"She's out to Bingo."

That sort of thing, it was sort of reassuring if you only thought with your heart instead of your brains. They could fall asleep but they were fools. Then Maddy didn't phone and they had to get up in the middle of the night.

"Go look for her, Jimmy," she said.

He drove all the way downtown.

"Don't lock the door," he said when he left.

There she was in the doughnut shop. No, that's not her. That's her. That's not her. That's her. Jimmy went in and Maddy came back out with him at two in the morning and they went home. Sullen, she was. It didn't make any sense, there was nothing they could do, there was no cause for this. They lay in bed and they saw Maddy all alone on some street in Halifax, somewhere they'd never been, Maddy still thinking she was some kind of Queen of the Ball.

The china anniversary, the twentieth year, by now all of that was blown over with Madeleine and she was back at school. She was fine. She had a boyfriend, Clyde Grandy. All her glitter makeup was thrown in the garbage can and gone.

"I think I'll sell the car, Rowena," he said.

"You don't have to do that," she said.

"We could use the money for something better, this is twenty years."

So he put his own ad in the paper and a guy came by and bought the car right off. "I sure loves this car, that colour," the guy said, "wait till the Missus sees this."

"Yes, just you wait," said Jimmy.

Then he went out and picked up the china servings, from the antique store. She'd already gone and made the choice.

"Don't drop it," the man said, "they break easy."

"But they're a hundred years old," said Jimmy, "they've been through lots."

"They break easy," the man said again, "china's like that."

On the way home, he drove slowly over the bumps, instead of pretending he could fly.

On the twenty-fifth anniversary he said, "There's no way we'll make fifty, that's rare."

"But they're in the paper all the time," she said, "we can hope for that too, just like they did."

"Okay," he said, "that's true, why not."

He bought her a silver brooch without her help.

Hey, she thought, he's getting better and better all the time at this.

One night in the thirty-seventh year of their marriage he woke up and said to her, "I got this headache."

He was covered in sweat. She got up and drove him to the hospital.

"He's fine," they said, in the Emergency Department, "but we'll keep him here a bit, make sure."

"Good," she said, "that's good, I'll go home, get his things."

"He'll be on the second floor," they said.

The phone rang when she was still at home.

"He's passed away," they said.

"What?"

"It happened so fast, my dear, there was nothing we could do, there was no suffering for him, no more than if he'd been in Halifax or Montreal, that we promise you."

All she could say was "Thanks, thanks for calling me."

What a thing to say, she thought later. She hung up the phone and put the bag down, the one with his pajamas.

Bury him in Mount Pearl? "No way," said Maddy, and they all agreed with her. They took him home to Belleoram in one of those hearses. The ground was still frozen. His brothers, the ones that were left, piled up tires in the old cemetery high on the hill, and they poured on spurts of gasoline, and they lit the match. The fire went on for hours. There were black lashings of smoke that crept and spilled across the Reach as far as Iron Skull, caught by the wind that would never stop that time of winter. The ground unfroze and they dug the grave. With thick gloves, four of them lowered the coffin down by ropes. She counted them up, seventeen people in all were there. The earth still smelled of burnt rubber, so she moved upwind to where Maddy was, standing there with her cousins, with Flo and Eunice, all three of them clinging together, dressed in black like crows. There was no choir of Angels and the sun never broke through the clouds. Clyde Grandy read a poem.

What kind of marriage was this anyway, everybody at the graveside wondered. Better than mine, better than yours? The same or different? It couldn't have been worse than the three of mine, one of them thought. Another said, they muddled through like we did. They were okay, they were nice as kids, they weren't wild. Now what's she going to do alone, there's room for me, another said to himself. Or: I don't know what to say about this. Or: Oh, she was sure pretty back then, look at her now, look at us all here in this sorry crowd. Finally: I could use a drink, my toes are gone as numb as the one in the casket there.

As for Maddy, she thought, they had a love like none she'd ever seen, the best. Maddy was the only one who really knew, the one that could be trusted. She was their witness. She was there for all the times, all the good, the bad, the useless times, the times between all those memory times, the nothing times, the times that added up to all their lives together. And the funny thing was, through it all, no one really seemed to reach out to make anything happen. It just did, it had a life of its own. That's how it was for them, for all of them, even after he died.

summer

THREE BUTTONS ON a blouse, a clavicle, a rib, an otherwise empty house, a dove on the windowsill (we'll call it that—shoo it away) the heat's like sap, those curtains, diaphanous, separate the air.

pivot

THEY LEARNED TO move like that in the kitchen when they were three and four and five, and if it weren't for the accordion and the one song they all knew and the uncle who was still in form back then, they never could have started with their feet and knees going like that like hammers, the notes slow at first but then it was picked up and without a break they stepped and danced until their eyes jigged and rattled in their own heads and they fell to the floor, they laughed, they reeled themselves out, the group was delirious, the arborite jumped, the pepper fell, the cocoa steamed, the door closed and then it was they stopped to breathe the same black wind out of the northeast, the white on white on black on black, the night waves on the Reach under the shadows of the biggest of the islands, the black sound the ocean made, the black shadow that moved on rocks, the black dog that came out of nowhere, the stars they knew so very few, the sound the grass made, the latch that froze or slipped or cried, the wood that cracked, the gate that swayed, the gravel scuffed, the rock they learned to pivot on before they learned to dance.

how kiziah got her baby

SHE KNEW SHE was turning into a mental case. In her mind, she ran through the way the sperm had looked under the doctor's microscope. They lay there lifeless. Plain as day, you could see there were millions of them. They were stacked there as thick as salt fish on those old archival photographs of flakes, but the trouble was, none of these sperm she looked at wiggled or thrashed or moved at all. Like the fish on those flakes, actually. And it wasn't supposed to be like that, for sperm.

"There's lots of them there all right," the doctor said, "but look, none of them wiggle. They're motionless. Also, some have two heads. You want to look, Mr. Buffett?"

"No thanks, I don't want to look, I believe you," said Cecil, "and I'm not scientifically inclined."

"He's in business," said Kiziah.

She could hardly blame Cecil for not looking. Who'd want to see that, all those lifeless sperm that came pulsing out of his own body? She wouldn't want to look, if she was the source of the problem.

"Two heads. That's bad?" she asked.

"Two heads, two tails, it's common enough but it's not good. There are a certain number of abnormal shapes in any ejaculate, Mrs. Buffett. That's normal, in nature, to have some faulty sperm morphology, but if there's a lot of abnormal shapes, a certain percentage, it gets in the way of the pregnancy process."

Sometimes, Kiziah thought she had two heads herself. One lived in the world the way it was but the other had on rose-coloured glasses, like the country-and-western song she and Cecil used to dance to, and that head, the rose-coloured one, kept hoping for something better.

It was small consolation that earlier that day, she'd got an A plus-plus herself in the physical check-up of her own body.

"You really got the perfect pelvis, Mrs. Buffett, a classic shape with lots of room, and your tubes are wide open. Patent, we call it. They're of the finest kind. The womb, the uterus, also nothing wrong there," the doctor said.

He snapped off his gloves.

"A plus-plus," he said.

"Is there a higher rating than that, than A plus-plus, Doctor?"

"In my scoring system, yes. There's triple-A, but that's reserved for those who've already conceived. At A plus-plus, or double-A, you're at the pinnacle of your own reference group, your own consort, that of healthy women who have not yet achieved pregnancy after a full calendar year of unprotected intercourse. Assuming a reasonable frequency."

The nurse who worked with the doctor was attractive, young, slender with dark shoulder-length hair and bright lipstick. A little more lipstick, Kiziah felt, than you'd expect for a woman in her position. A nurse. Like she was dressed up for a cocktail party, rather than clinical work. She bent down towards Kiziah.

"There you go, my dear," she said, "that's good news for you. You're fine."

"So, frequency of coitus," said the doctor, "How many times a week, in your estimation, do you and your husband have sexual intercourse?"

Kiziah looked at Cecil. She blushed.

"Three, four times," she said.

There was no harm in exaggerating. After all, that's how they started out and it was only recently that they'd tailed off. Once a week was more like it now but why tell these doctors everything? Julia, her older sister, had sex just once, the very first time, and even though she wasn't sure what happened to her, *bang* she was pregnant. And now, Julia's happy as can be.

"That's more than enough, three or four times a week," said the doctor.

"Some do it just once a week," said the nurse, "that's not considered a good effort."

She looked at the doctor for confirmation. He nodded his head.

Sure, it was good news, the A plus-plus pelvis, the open Fallopian tubes, and the anatomically correct uterus. Thank God for small mercies. She was ready and waiting for a miracle now, ready to put on the rose-coloured glasses.

But then they sent Cecil off, privately, into another room with only a glass jar and a brown lunch bag.

"Go in there, make sure you lock the door. Read the instructions," the doctor said to Cecil. "You get the sample by masturbation. No lubricants. No spilling. Keep it warm too, once you got it. Hold the specimen bottle under your arm. There's magazines in there, if you need help."

Cecil pointed to the indicated door and looked at his wife.

"Magazines?" he said, "I don't think I'll need those."

"You'd be surprised," said the doctor, "it's not like at home. The atmosphere here is very clinical."

Then Cecil went into the next room and closed the door with a click. He seemed to be in there a long, long time, and when he came out, he looked sheepish, standing there with the bag. Then he put the bag under his arm, as he'd been told, and held it there against his chest.

The poor guy, Kiziah thought, that's not easy for him, in a place like this.

Right away, the nurse called back the doctor and the doctor had a look at Cecil's specimen. He measured the total amount in a small syringe, and then ejected a little bit of it onto a glass slide.

"Volume five cc's, good," he said.

The nurse wrote it down on a form.

"That's lots," she said to Kiziah.

"We need to look at it right away, while it's still warm from the body," said the doctor. "That's how we judge motility. The more motility, the better, needless to say."

He sat down at the microscope and focused the eyepiece up and down.

"Hmm, look at this, please, nurse."

The nurse walked over and looked into the microscope. She had to brush away that long dark hair to have a look. To balance herself better, without sitting down, she put one hand on the doctor's shoulder. Kiziah noticed her manicured fingernails, smooth and perfect. The nurse looked for a minute and then stood back up then and looked at the doctor and then she looked at Cecil.

"I'm not the expert," she said.

"Lots and lots of sperm there, lots of them," the doctor said.

Later, Kiziah wondered why he said it like that. It must be how they break bad news. They perk you up with a spark of hope. Maybe they teach doctors that. "There's no sign of cancer in your lung, sir," they'd say, "but of course there is cancer in your brain, your heart, your liver, and your leg and you got a week to live."

"Take a look now, Mrs. Buffett, what do you see?"

"I could never see anything through those, in school," she said.

"Oh, it's easy. These are much better microscopes. Put your eye right here, adjust this, up and down a bit. You'll see them."

And it was easy, there were many small head shapes with tails everywhere she looked. Her heart took a leap, like a salmon fighting its way upstream.

"Oh! I see sperm, lots of them! Cecil, good for you!"

Cecil smiled. He was pleased, she could tell.

"Oh yes, there are lots," the doctor said.

"Yes," said the nurse.

Now, if Kiziah sold, say, woolen gloves for a living—as once she did—and she opened up a new package of woolen gloves when they came into the store, and she saw, right away, that there were moth holes in each and every pair, what would she say? Would she say to the customer standing there, "Lots of woolen gloves here, Mrs. Whittle, lots of fine wool?" No, she didn't think so. She'd say, "Oh, what a shame, these gloves are ridden with moth holes. These gloves are eaten up, they're no good at all, they're useless for warmth." That's what she'd say, she knew that. But no, this doctor said, "Lots of sperm, there are lots of sperm." Then he paused, the nurse took her look, the doctor looked back down the microscope again, adjusted the eyepiece a quarter-turn, shifted the slide here and there, and then he came out with the truth that he'd known all along.

"But this is not good: none of these sperm wiggle," the doctor said.

"Wiggle?" asked Kiziah.

"Motility is important. Spermatozoa should move, they should be vigorous, they should be pulsing with life, their tails should thrash as they probe their way towards the ready egg."

"You mean there's something wrong?" asked Kiziah.

Again her heart like the salmon leapt in her chest, upriver.

"Look again, Mrs. Buffett, and this time don't just look for the sperm, watch for movement too."

That's when she had her second look, and she saw them all there again but they looked dead. She'd seen tadpoles like that once, in a ditch on Waterford Bridge Road where the water had an oily scum.

"Maybe they're in a pause," she said, "catching their wind after that journey they had."

That was the rose-coloured glasses talking. The doctor and the nurse both laughed, spontaneously, naturally.

"No, I'm afraid not," the doctor said, "they don't rest on these slides. After a journey like that, all the way through the seminiferous tubules, from the distant testicles, sperm are frisky. If healthy, they're like colts out of the barn on a spring day."

The nurse looked at the doctor and turned to Cecil.

"Mr. Buffett, look at it this way: it's like you shake up a can of Coca-Cola. The ejaculation of spermatozoa is an energy release, a life force that spews out. Our job as scientists, here, is to measure the effectiveness of that energy release."

"There's no sperm in Coca-Cola," said Cecil.

"Of course not," said the nurse, "and really, unfortunately, there are no viable sperm, it appears, on your specimen either."

She pointed to the microscope. The doctor looked about twenty-eight years old. The nurse? Maybe thirty.

"I'm afraid that's right," said the doctor. "But a better analogy might be, say, ejaculation is like shaking up or squeezing a milkweed pod, shaking it, squeezing it, watching the million seeds fly everywhere into the wind. Catch those seeds, look at them under the microscope, that's what our job is like."

He looked at the Buffetts, hoping they understood. Of course they understood.

"But wait, milkweed's dry," said the nurse, "and sperm itself is carried in a liquid propulsive medium."

NICHOLAS RUDDOCK

She laughed gently and shook her hair again. She was standing right beside the doctor, her right hip pretty much touching his left shoulder. Cecil stood on the other side of the room, and Kiziah could see how deflated he was, downcast. He had his brave face on, though, but she could tell. She probably had the same face on herself. She loved him, she always had.

"Well, let's put it this way then," said the doctor, "to be successful, the procreative act has to have living seeds. And lots of them, Mr. and Mrs. Buffett, lots of them. Millions, millions, hundreds of millions. Active spermatozoa are the living seeds of *homo sapiens*. Unfortunately, this sample of Mr. Buffett's is severely deficient in that department."

The doctor put his hand on the nurse's back, and he left it there for a second.

"If you put a red tomato on the floor," said the nurse, "and then you hit that tomato as hard as you can with a sledgehammer, then you have wet seeds flying all over. High speed. That's what the male fertilization process is like. Sperm are ejaculated at twenty miles an hour."

"That's a good analogy," said the doctor, "but for the fact that the explosion of seminal fluid happens, usually, within an enclosed space, the female vagina."

"Of course," said the nurse.

They seemed to be talking to each other now, rather than to the Buffetts.

"That's why condoms," said the doctor.

"What? Condoms? What's that got to do with this?" interjected Kiziah.

"Condoms prevent pregnancy," the doctor said.

There was a pause.

Then the doctor looked at Kiziah and said, "What I mean, Mrs. Buffett, is that young unattached people, people attracted to each other, wear condoms for protection from disease as well as for the prevention of an unwanted pregnancy. This is of no concern for you today, for you and your husband, because we are in a fertility clinic, the purpose of which is quite the opposite. The nurse and I have mentioned condoms only to contextualize the whole fertility process, as we understand it. No doubt you have used condoms in the past."

"Not for two years," said Kiziah.

She felt numb inside. All those dead sperm.

"You, a married couple, trying to get pregnant, Mrs. Buffett, should not concern yourself with condoms. Condoms are for single women."

The doctor and nurse glanced at each other. Maybe Kiziah imagined it. Cecil had his back against the wall, by the door.

"Let's go, Kiziah," he said.

The nurse broke away from her satellite position around the doctor, crossed the room and patted Cecil on the shoulder.

"There, there," she said, "we never give up on just one sample. Come back next week, Mr. Buffett, try again. Results like this, it could be a fluke. It could be better next time. Make an appointment at the desk."

"You mean do this again?" asked Cecil.

"No relations for three days, then try again. It's the only way to be sure of the diagnosis."

"Diagnosis?"

"Well," she said, "I'm afraid, if we get the same results again, we diagnose male infertility."

"Seedless red tomatoes you mean," said Kiziah, "we smash your so-called red tomato against the ground with your so-called sledgehammer and nothing of much use flies out."

"Maybe we shouldn't have made those comparisons," said the doctor.

"Maybe not," said Kiziah.

"It's how we help people understand. Male infertility is common."

"It's how you belittle people," said Kiziah.

The nurse formed her lips into a tight line. The doctor stood up. Kiziah took Cecil's arm and they left the clinic and walked out into the parking lot. Three days of abstinence and then another sperm count? They could do that, she figured, even for those unfeeling health so-called professionals. Fuck them. She and Cecil didn't have much choice. Those two were the only ones in the city dealing with those who didn't yet have babies.

On the way home, Cecil was quiet behind the wheel. He didn't whistle *Whiskey in the Jar* and he didn't whistle the theme song from *Titanic*.

"What do you think, honey?" she said.

"I'm sorry about all those dead sperm, Kizie, that's what I think."

"It's not your fault, you heard what they said. It's common."

"My sperm are duds. They're useless."

"No, no, not useless. You never know. Now we take three days off, next week we try again. Like the nurse said, sometimes it's better."

"She's a piece of work, that nurse. And we had five days off this time."

"Five? Three. It was only three."

"Well, five, three, what's the difference? I'm supposed to go through that rigmarole again? I don't think so."

She smiled at him, leaned over, tapped his thigh.

"Cecil, it's the only way, for us."

"I'm not going back there, Kiziah. There's no way. That's it. The doctor, the nurse, they laugh way too much. I could have died back there."

Wait a minute, wait a minute she thought. She turned in her seat and looked right at him.

"Cecil, when you went into that little room, the sample room?"

"Oh Kiziah, please."

"Was there anyone else there, Cecil, any other men getting their samples at the same time? Any chance of a mix-up?"

"God no, I was there alone. They had a latch on the door for God sake. A lock inside."

"Were there any other jars? Sperm jars?"

"Empty ones lined up by the toilet. Empty ones on a ledge. Empty ones."

"Cec, maybe, when you finished, I bet you put that little bottle with your sperm sample down somewhere."

Cecil thought about what he'd done.

"That's true," he said, "I had to put it up on the ledge, to do up my belt. So what?"

"Well maybe that's when the mix-up happened. You put yours down, you picked up someone else's, someone's full of dead sperms, duds, leftovers from before, cold as ice. No wonder they didn't move."

Cecil was quiet. He thought about his wife, how much she wanted a baby.

"That's not impossible," he said, "maybe that's not impossible. If they have no standards of cleanliness or scientific rigour, Kizie, if they have no fail-safe procedures, if they should be disbarred from the practice of medicine, that is possible."

There you go. She could find the silver lining anywhere. That's why he'd fallen for her in the first place. Nothing got her down for long.

"There was a switch of sperm, Cecil," she said.

He thought about the other two girls he'd had sex with before Kiziah. Neither of them ever got pregnant either. There were lots of times they could have too, times they got carried away and did not use condoms. They thought they were lucky then, not to have had a baby come along, mess up their lives.

"I mean they even switch real babies by accident sometimes. Let alone sperm. I read about it," said Kiziah. "Missus So-and-So, down the steps of the hospital with her brand-new little baby, happy as a clam. Then three months later, the phone call comes. Bring that baby back, there's been a mix-up."

Cecil said nothing. He knew the dead sperms under the microscope were his. The bottle he'd taken back to the doctor was warm at the bottom, the warmth surprised him, it came up through the palm of his hand and made him feel like an alien, like he didn't know much about anything at all. Particularly about himself.

"We'll go back, Cecil, we have to. Do it again. Make sure it's your jar this time, keep hold of it, don't ever put it down."

"Okay," he said.

But he knew he'd never go back to that place, never have another one of those tests, never masturbate in a closet, never hear that doctor and that nurse mock them both while he stood there, shamed.

"You know what they'll say to us, next time?"

"No, Cecil, what will they say?"

"They'll say 'Take any kind of fruit you want, Mr. Buffett, grind it up in a Cuisinart, throw that mess of seeds into a pressure hose, a hundred million seeds fly out,' and then the nurse will say, 'Oh and the tighter the landing space, the warmer the better,' and those two will look at each other and laugh and she'll throw her hair around. To hell with them."

"All you need is one or two alive, I think, Cec. They can take those, pull them out and use them. There's test-tubes, they got their ways."

Kiziah already felt better. Again she thought about the unlucky mothers who came down the stairs outside the hospital with the wrong baby. She thought about Cecil coming out of the sample room, smiling this time. She saw herself nine months later lying on her back in the delivery room, bright lights up above, and she squeezed Cecil's hand because of the pain coming through her in waves. Now there were different doctors, nice doctors with green masks hovering over her like they were the best friends she ever had. They didn't tell jokes, they cared for her. Sweat poured off her face and trickled down the side of her neck. She was born for this. So what, it hurts. "Push, push," the nurse said, and then there was the baby coming out. "It's a boy! It's twins!" Who'd think of that? That didn't show on the ultrasound! How crazy is that? Then they held the two babies up by the feet, and gave them a smack on the bottom and they all started to cry, including Cecil. So much for the dead sperm, she whispered into his ear as he bent down to give her another kiss, what did those scientists know anyway?

She couldn't wait for it all to happen. That night she cozied up to Cecil who was lying there, quiet on his back. She moved herself up against him and wiggled back and forth against his hip.

"What am I?" she said.

"Beats me."

"I'm an egg just out of the ovary. Grade A plus-plus."

It was a dark night and she couldn't see his face so she lifted herself up to look.

"Let's wait the three nights," he said, "give me a chance. That's what the doctor said."

"Let's do it now too. For fun."

"Kiziah."

"Cecil?"

"Kizie, I'm tired out. I'm sampled out. There's a limit to what I can do."

He turned away from her. There was a cold spot on her shoulders where the sheets pulled away.

All those spermatozoa, they couldn't have been born dead,

they couldn't have been lifeless from the word go. Something happened, something sucked the living spirit out of them, something beat them down, flattened them out, grew the two heads, the two tails, caused the slow or sudden death that made them useless. Maybe he had his limits, Cecil, maybe he was tired and worn out and disappointed but there were no limits for her, for Kiziah Buffett. She'd have her baby no matter what. She was on a mission. She fell asleep with that in mind.

Two days later she almost made a mistake. She was in the Honda Civic, alone, and she nearly got killed on the highway. There she was, she had the accelerator put to the floor, all the weight of her hip and her leg on it, pushing hard. Nothing much happened. There was no acceleration. No roar like a tiger from the engine, her body wasn't drilled back into the upholstery. In fact, she was hung out to dry in the passing lane, with fog closing down in front, zero visibility, the truck beside her full-blast full of steel rods whipping up spray all over her windshield. So she had a quick choice to make: keep this up and get killed, or pull back. She put on the brakes and backed off just in time because a cement mixer came by the other way. She could have been a bug on the grill.

"Useless car, not really safe," she said that night to Cecil.

And what did he say? "It's good on gas. You need to learn self-control."

"I could have got killed, Cecil. It's got no guts, no get up and go. No safety reserve."

"It's a great car, it's good on gas, it has re-sale value. You should never have tried to pass under those conditions. You have to learn."

That was all he said, and it was obvious to her that he did not see, in his mind's eye, his wife, Kiziah, out there in that car, the car gasping in the passing lane, the cement mixer coming her way, disguised by fog, ready to kill her. He didn't have the imagination to see it and feel it, to vibrate with it the way she did.

So she said; and she knew she shouldn't, "Cecil, day after tomorrow's the day for the next sperm count. You got to go for that."

He walked out of the room and didn't say a thing. They always talked things out before. She followed him.

"I can drive you there first thing," she said.

"Kiziah, I love you but I am never going back to that place, ever. I am not going to do it."

She could hardly breathe.

"Jesus, Cecil, I'd lie down naked in front of City Hall for a chance for a baby."

"Well go ahead, just let me know if you do, I don't want to be there."

He walked out the door. The Honda started up and drove away. It was true, she thought, you didn't need much acceleration here on Empire Avenue, there was not much of a hill, not much traffic. Puttering around in the Honda was okay most of the time.

She went upstairs and took her temperature. There was the little spike that showed ovulation. No surprise, she was like clockwork, day thirteen or fourteen of every cycle, pop out came the egg. She could have had a hundred babies by now, with the right sperm. Like the doctor said, her body was A plus-plus. She looked at herself in the mirror.

Go for it.

That evening, after a dinner of turkey with dressing and a pie she made herself, she said, "Cecil, I might stay out later than usual tonight."

"The card group?"

"Mary Lou's."

"Sure, honey, go ahead, I got this book to read. Oh, by the way, I made arrangements, I'm trading in the Honda."

"You are?"

"I figured it out, the gas isn't that great after all."

"No?"

"No. A Mustang, that's what we're going to have. By tomorrow".

"More pep in one of those, right?"

"That's putting it lightly. It's like a rocket. Pass anything, anywhere. The gas is surprisingly good too. That's why I thought, I might as well."

She went over to him and sat on the arm of his chair. She bent down and kissed the side of his neck.

"This A plus-plus body of mine, and thus this body of yours, too, Cecil, is, according to scientific measurements, ovulating right now. Time to test out those sperm of yours under ideal conditions. All we need is one little guy, you know, not a hundred million."

He kissed her. He slipped his hand under her sweater. They went upstairs to the bedroom and took off all their clothes. They were in a hurry, so full of desire they were. He fell on top of her and entered her and she felt him come in spasms.

"I think we did it, Cecil."

He was still breathing fast.

"I know we did, I know we did."

She wrapped her legs up and around him, holding him inside.

"Stay in me," she said. "Remember this date."

An hour later, she kissed Cecil again and went out the door for Mary Lou's. But she didn't go there, she stopped the Civic just before the corner of Empire Avenue and Rennie's Mill Road and pulled out her cellphone.

"Mary Lou? Kiziah. I won't make it tonight after all. Cecil's sick, I'm staying home. Call Cindy, she'll pitch in. Okay? Sorry."

Then she drove to Duckworth Street and found a parking spot. She walked down the short steps to George Street. It was ten o'clock by then and the bars were hopping. She walked into one of them, any one would do. She could move on if she had to. She stood at the bar and had one drink and a second one, ten minutes later. Screwdrivers. That's what she always had at Mary Lou's. She felt nervous, almost the same as she did in the passing lane with the fog and the cement truck coming her way. But this time she kept her foot down on the gas.

"One more of these here screwdrivers, please."

The man three down from her? About the same build as Cecil, maybe five years younger, by himself. He looked at her. He raised his glass.

Was this bad for babies, all these drinks of alcohol, these screwdrivers? Don't think so. Julia's baby was perfect. Julia said she was loaded the night it happened to her. Couldn't remember a damn thing. What's she got now? A lifetime of love.

The man down the bar came over to her. He touched her shoulder carefully and said something. She couldn't make it out for some reason, the noise, the music, the chatter, harsh laughter all around them. Get it over, Kiziah.

She put her hand on the young stranger's arm, moved her lips up by his ear.

"Barb," she shouted, "that's my name."

That was her name for the baby, if it was a girl. Barbara.

Again he said something, again she couldn't hear him.

Undeterred, caution to the wind, she shouted again.

"You know out the Battery, past the old guns?"

He looked at her, he nodded. He must have heard her. He bent to her.

"I know that spot," he said. "Why?"

She was getting used to the noise. His voice came through now.

"There's a nice patch of grass out there, if you're game," she said.

So that's how Kiziah Buffett got her baby. Sure, she loved her husband. In fact she loved him so much she took off her rose-coloured glasses, took off her clothes from the waist down and laid back in the wet grass past the old guns. And she never told anybody, never told Cecil, never told Barbara, blotted it out of her mind, and who's going to condemn her for that?

No one, not me, that's for sure.

the steamer

SHORTLY AFTER CLYDE'S twin sister, that sweet girl, Meta Maud Grandy, left town for Halifax, Aaron Stoodley began to send her letters. He was in love with her but he didn't know it. He thought he just wanted to talk. As for her, she never gave Aaron Stoodley a thought even when the letters started to roll in. That was because she never got a single one. Each and every letter was steamed open, read and tucked away by the man she'd moved in with. His name was Harold Butts, and he made seventy dollars an hour as a deep-sea diver, and that was more dollars per hour than all the Grandys, put together, ever got. Maybe that turned Meta Maud's head a bit. He was a good-looking guy, Harold Butts, and when he pulled off his wetsuit he had hair all over his chest. Not like Aaron, who was skinny as a rabbit. Aaron did not write long letters but there was something in them anyway that bothered Harold Butts.

Dear Meta Maud, Aaron wrote the first time. *Things are good here for the most part. Every day I walk up and down Barter's Hill. Clyde's doing okay at the bakery so far, I think.*
  Aaron.

The deep-sea diver steamed open that letter with the kettle on low. Meta Maud was asleep upstairs. What could he have thought? That's no love letter, he must have said to himself. Who's this Aaron Stoodley anyway? After Harold Butts read it through five times, he sealed up the envelope again using a glue jar and a flat wooden stick that came from a popsicle. Then he went down to the basement, turned on the light, and he put Aaron Stoodley's first letter away in the dark, deep down inside the oldest diving bag he had. She'd never look there in a million years, she wasn't the curious type.

That night, over fish and chips down the street at Al's, he said to her, "What's the names of all those friends of yours back home?" He was so casual, he still had food in his mouth. And Meta Maud said to herself, Why that's nice, he's never asked much. She could overlook the food. She said, "Well there's Eunice Cluett who's my best friend, and Eunice, her friend is Henry, and then there's Aaron Stoodley." "What's he like?" said Harold Butts. "Who, Aaron?" said Meta Maud, "he's just Aaron, he's nice, makes you laugh. That's all."

Dear Meta Maud, he wrote the second time. *Things are good here. There's lots of rain, which is no big surprise. Clyde's first paycheck, he's happy. There's a waterpipe broken on Barter's Hill, it made a real mess downtown. You'd have to wear your boots to keep dry.*

Aaron.

Now what did Aaron Stoodley mean by that? Aaron didn't know and neither did Harold Butts, who read it. But if you knew Aaron better than either of them did, that's a love letter for sure. Barter's Hill was the road he walked on with Meta Maud Grandy every day, down to where she worked. Nights he'd meet her again, walk her back up the hill no matter when. Just friends they were, and Aaron said he liked the workout. They'd talk up and down the hill, mostly about Clyde. He sure had problems, Clyde did. Aaron never wrote one letter to Meta Maud without putting in it, somewhere at least, Barter's Hill, and Clyde.

Harold Butts steamed this second one open too and read it five times. Whoever this Aaron was, the letters didn't make much sense. Sure wasn't longwinded. He never said *I love you lots*, or *Your passionate friend*, or *Miss you*. There was nothing there like that, flat-out nothing at all. Harold knew who Clyde was, he didn't worry a second about Clyde, her no-good brother, the twin who couldn't do much. The deep-sea diver went down to the basement and put the second letter into the same bag. Those letters to Meta Maud, they cozied up in the dark against the picture magazines he had hidden in there. No harm to that, everybody had their magazines. Anyway, lucky for him, he had the kettle trick down pat, kept it on low and real quiet. Got real slick at it. Meta Maud, why he liked her lots. She read books, she talked up a storm, she made friends easy.

Dear Meta Maud Grandy, this was Aaron's third letter. *I hope you don't mind these, all the letters. Everything's still fine and dandy here. Eunice and Henry, they're fine, they don't know I've taken my pen in hand. They'd laugh. No letters from you but don't worry, one-way's fine. Clyde's okay at the bakery, but they've moved him down near the coffee machine. That might be a mistake. I'll walk him down to work, remind him what we said about the job he blew, back at Tim's, with the coffee. Hey Meta Maud, Barter's Hill looks the same, still up one way and down the other.*

Harold Butts put the kettle on low again. That way, the whistle never came on and wouldn't wake her up but what the heck, she slept deep anyway, you could shout and dance most of the time. Then he steamed open the envelope. First he laid the steam at one edge and moved along. The hard part was by the stamp. If there was too much steam put there, the stamp crinkled up and you could tell. Thirty seconds was all it took, he was fast. He wondered what the world record was, anyway, for steaming letters on the sly. Then he laughed at that and thought to himself,

Never see that one in the Guinness Book.

Then, after he read through the whole thing, it didn't take long, he thought, that silly Clyde Grandy? Hopeless case, you ask me. Why bother writing about a loser like that? Worst thing about the letters, it was boring. Hey wait a minute, wait a minute, maybe they're after pulling a fast one here, maybe there's a secret message. *Yours*, that was new. He didn't like that. Maybe there's a K-I-S-S-E-S or a S-E-X in there, only she could see. The first letter in each word maybe, check it out. Harold laid the letter from the retard flat out and looked for clues. Then oh my, he heard the bed creak upstairs and there were footsteps. "Hi there, honey, the kettle's on, you're up too early, go on back to bed, you need your sleep, there's nothing here, I just got the bills."

Jeez, that was close I must say. Always have a spare tank Harold, when you go down deep like that. There's no buddies down here. Now. There we go, take the first letter each line. He picked up his pen with the purple ink and he circled the first letter in every line and he did that to all the old letters too. Now at least they looked good, full of colour.

Twenty minutes later Harold Butts gave up. There was no secret message. No darlings, no kisses that he could find, and the way that Aaron Stoodley wrote, he was like a simpleton with no brains. Like that twin brother of hers, that Clyde, they made a fine pair. Down he went to the basement and put the third letter in the dark bag. He was a fox all right, he was a deep-sea diver and there was no telling how far down he could go. That's what he thought to himself on the way back upstairs.

Dear Meta Maud (letter number four) *I don't know about your brother now. Down the hill I went to the bakery, and there was Clyde making coffee. He had the sweat popped out all over him. Then he poured all the coffee out at once, all of it down the drain. Right away, he made a new pot. It was like at Tim's all over again. He looked*

around, down the drain it went, surreptitiously. I was the only one who saw it, I'm pretty sure. Then he made up a third pot right away. That's no good for Clyde. He hasn't overcome that fixation of his. They find out, he's gone. Maybe answer me this time please, Meta Maud.
Best as always,
Yours,
Aaron.

Fat chance she'd ever answer, thought Harold Butts.

Three weeks later, he and Meta Maud went out to The Keg. They had a special dinner for what they called their two-month anniversary. By then he must have had twenty letters from Aaron Stoodley, all of them sequestered in the diving bag. That night at The Keg, he had a lot more wine than he was used to, but what the heck, she had the keys to the car, she could be the driver. Steak and baked potatoes and after that it was apple pie. What a time they had. "Remember the dance we met," he said, "you was so shy back then." And Meta Maud smiled and agreed and then the waitress came by and she said, "You folks want coffee?" and Harold laughed and said to Meta Maud, "Hey, honey, why not? Maybe your crazy brother Clyde fixed it up." And Meta Maud said, "Fixed what up? What did Clyde fix up?" "The coffee, the coffee," he said with a big laugh, "Clyde fixed up the coffee!" So Meta Maud laughed, sort of, and they drove home and at 2 a.m. she woke up with a chill in the middle of her heart and said, "Whoa, wait a minute, I never said anything at all to Harold about Clyde and coffee. Where'd he get that idea from?" "Harold," she said, "wake up. Harold, where'd you get that about Clyde and coffee?" He was half-asleep. "You told me, you told me about the coffee. Meta Maud, go back to sleep." So she did go back to sleep, and in the morning, first thing, she poured the orange juice for him and off he went down to the harbour. "Some big steel rods fell off the barge," he said, "seventy dollars an hour for me. What's twelve times seventy? See you in eight hundred and forty dollars." Off he went and Meta Maud Grandy sat there. What the hell, what the hell, what the hell, she thought. Then: let's figure it out. Phone home.

Back on Fitzpatrick Avenue, Eunice Cluett and Henry Fiander were already in a bit of a funk when they heard the phone ring. The problem Eunice and Henry had, and they'd had it for some time, was none other than Aaron Stoodley himself, and the problem with Aaron Stoodley was that he'd turned into a zombie. Always on the couch. He lay there like a washed-up giant squid. Every time they walked by, they had to say, "Move those tentacles please, move those tentacles." Then he'd shift a bit but otherwise, when they said, "What's wrong with you, Aaron Stoodley?" he couldn't seem to muster up an answer. He seemed to have no strength. This was a big change, because up till then he was a house on fire all the time. More likely they had to say, "Close the damper down some, Aaron, you'll wear out like one of those supernovas." Now, with Meta Maud gone a couple months or more, there he was, a zombie on the couch. Paralyzed. They had no idea that he'd sent twenty letters off to Meta Maud, and received none back at all.

The phone rang.

"Get the phone, Aaron, please," said Eunice.

She had Queenie in her lap, and a book.

"I can't. I'm de-oxygenated."

That was the word he used for the disease he figured he had, the one that made him tired all the time. A big medical book lay on the floor by the couch, and when Henry picked it up one day, it fell open to the page that said *Leukemia*. "This what you got?" he asked Aaron. "That's it, I got it all." Henry read a bit more and said, "You got loss of appetite, weight loss, sweats in the night and chest pains?" To that Aaron said, "I don't have every single one of those, Henry, but I got most of them. And I'm de-oxygenated. My oxygen bubbles are way too few. My muscles are thus starved of life-giving oxygen. It's leukemia, I'm almost sure." Then Eunice went over to the couch and snapped up the book from the dying man. She leafed through it a bit, gave it back and said, "Aaron, read this, right here. Where it says *Depression*." "Depression?" "That's what you got, you poor guy, but that's all you got. You're pining away. I've seen it lots of times. Jump up and live."

But he lay on the couch anyway, he didn't believe her.

Eunice put Queenie down and ran for the phone herself.

"Hello," she said, and then she laughed out loud. "Why girl, you fell off the earth."

Then Eunice was real quiet, listening.

Finally she said, "Things aren't so good here right now, Meta Maud. Clyde's gone and messed up and lost the job at the bakery. Aaron's dying on the couch. Otherwise, we're fine and dandy."

Aaron Stoodley stood up.

"Talk to Aaron, though. He's right here. He's the one who really knows about Clyde. He kept an eye on him, for all the good it did."

She held the phone up in the air like it was a prize and waved it and said, "Aaron, oh Aaron, it's Miss Meta Maud Grandy all the way from the big city of Halifax, just for you."

All of a sudden the man with the fatal De-oxygenating Leukemia Disease jumped up from the couch and came into the kitchen and took the phone from Eunice Cluett.

"Meta Maud? It's you?"

He was so weak from Leukemia that his hand and his voice trembled.

"It's me all right. Aaron, what's up with Clyde?"

"He didn't make it, Meta Maud, he didn't pull it off."

"The coffee again?"

"That's it. Fixated on making it. It'd be laughable under other circumstances."

"Aaron, you should've let me know, we probably could have done something."

"I wrote you the letters, Meta Maud. There was nothing else I could do."

"Letters?"

"Twenty letters."

"You did? That was sweet of you. But I didn't get any."

They checked the address and there was no mistake there.

"Well, we'll deal with that later," she said. "Tell me what happened."

"Simple enough. The first few days Clyde was fine. He made the coffee right, he walked away. He swept up the floor. He cut the bread. He tied on the little tags for the jam. Just like we showed him. But then he started to watch the coffee all the time, a bad omen. Like he did at Tim's. I warned him over and over. But you know Clyde, he's weird now and then. That was it."

"That was it?"

"Pretty much. One day he made twenty pots of coffee five minutes apart, pouring most of it down the drain, when he thought no one was looking."

"He did that on purpose."

"Maybe."

"He didn't want that job."

"Maybe."

"I don't know what we can do."

"It's nice to hear your voice, Meta Maud."

"He still seeing the doughnut girl?"

"Yes he is. That's going fine. How's your diver, Meta Maud?"

Aaron knew she had a deep-sea diver now because, in the one postcard Meta Maud sent to Eunice, she said so. It wasn't easy to ask.

"I'm not so sure about him, the diver," she said.

Then Meta Maud, before she hung up the phone, said something like, "It's nice to talk to you again, Aaron Stoodley."

That's what he remembered of the phone call.

"You sent Meta Maud Grandy letters, Aaron Stoodley, you fox, all behind our back?" asked Eunice.

"Someone had to keep her up to date. But she didn't get them."

"My, who's in love with who, I wonder now," said Eunice.

She said it real softly so no one could hear, but later on that day, when they were all alone, she said to Henry Fiander, "Aaron's in love."

"Meta Maud?"

"That's the one. He's been sending her letters, and he can't breathe or move when she's away."

"Too bad he's got the fatal De-oxygenating Leukemia Disease, beyond the help of doctors. That's bad timing for him."

"You saw him run out of here after that phone call?"

"I did, he had his tentacles going in the right direction, for the first time in weeks."

"Oxygenated. I tell you, he's cured by a miracle."

After she hung up the phone, Meta Maud Grandy sat there at the kitchen table in Halifax. Nice condo they had, that's for sure. Harold Butts, he was gone for the full twelve-hour shift. He was probably, right now, pulling on the wetsuit and putting on the big helmet before he pushed off backwards, off the Zodiac. She'd watched him do it. Down he went with the big chains. He said you could hardly see down there, in the murk of the harbour. That's what he called it, the murk of the harbour. "Like going down into a dark basement, honey, you can't see zip down there. Mostly you hear yourself breathe in and out, and you feel your way around a lot with the gloves, they're big and thick." Apparently, they lowered lights down there to penetrate the murk of the harbour. Hours, it took hours to wrap the chains on whatever they had to pull up, to do it right. Today it was iron bars. You had to be a certain kind to do that, and that's why they paid him so well.

THE STEAMER

"Ha-ha-ha," that's what she remembered, the night before at The Keg.

"Ha-ha-ha."

The way he laughed out loud.

"Maybe it was your twin brother, Meta Maud, maybe it was your Clyde made the coffee. Hey, I'll have some of that coffee, sweetie."

And that was the waitress he talked to when he said that, when he said sweetie. Only one way he could have known about Clyde and coffee; he must have read the letters that were meant for her. What did he do then, burn them up? What was he? Some kind of creep like on TV? What did she know, she was only eighteen years old. Hair all over his chest, so what, screw him, she thought.

Well what the hell, Mister Harold Butts? Gone twelve hours now, that's for sure. Where are the letters? Gone for good? He kicked around a lot in the basement. She could do that, she could dive down, rattle some chains, and penetrate the murk of the harbour of the creep. Might find what he called zip, might find lots, you never knew.

She got up and she flicked on the cellar light and down she went, clump-clump, she heard her own footsteps in the quiet, dead as night. There wasn't much down there. "This won't take long, Meta Maud," she said.

Over there, a set of golf clubs, over there, the bags she brought from home. Then there was a set of filing cabinets, and in the far corner a loose pile of bags—sports bags and luggage bags and diving bags all in a clump. The filing cabinet was empty. All it did was wobble and creak. Goldilocks, I'm like her. What now? The bags, the diving bags of Mr. Deep-sea Diver, that's next, so she moved them with her foot and what do you know, one of those bags was full. This one here, buried at the bottom of the pile. She picked it up and loosened the thin rope that kept it closed at one end, and she put her hand inside. Well, Goldilocks, let's go upstairs with the evidence. Clump-clump, up into the morning light she went, and two miles away, Mister Harold Butts adjusted his mouthpiece. Time for the very first dive on what looked like the finest kind of day.

First thing she did, Meta Maud, was to pour herself some orange juice in a glass, and then she emptied out the diving bag, all of it, onto the kitchen table. Then she sat down and looked. Naked magazines, he had plenty of those all right. They made up most of the weight of the bag. But then there was a pack of letters tied up with a big elastic, the kind of elastic you get on the mail sometime.

Let's see.

Sure enough, the little packet, and every envelope was the same. It said on the top left corner, From *Mister Aaron Stoodley, 7 Fitzpatrick Avenue, St. John's, Newfoundland.* There you go, judge and jury, guilty as sin. The twenty letters, why, it looked like they'd never been opened. That made no sense. She took a closer look; the edges of the envelopes were all smeared with glue. She put her hand down farther into the diving bag and felt around and out she came with a small glue jar. Elmer's Glue, like they used to have in kindergarten. Whatever made him do this? He'd gone and piled up the letters meant for her, smack up against his dirty magazines. You want to stay with a man like that, Meta Maud? Someone who opened your mail? Someone who glued it up again? She took her letters and examined them; they were all numbered in purple ink on the outside of the envelopes. That's his work, he owned a whole slew of those coloured pens. "These never leak," he'd said. She opened one of the envelopes at random. Even more weird, he'd gone and circled the first letter of every line with his purple ink pen. Then he'd made a list of all those single letters, trying to make up words, as though solving a puzzle. He's looking for secret messages. My God.

THE STEAMER

Meta Maud had all day, she had no classes till late afternoon. Down in the harbour, he might be up by now, off the air tanks. "Never stay down too long, that's the secret," he said. Not the only secret he's got, apparently. Make your own secrets, Harold Butts, instead of stealing mine.

She read the letters one by one, in order.

The last one: *Dear Meta Maud, Clyde's home three weeks now with nothing on the horizon. We're wracking our brains, and that's not easy. We need you, Meta Maud, to give us a call. We need to pick your brain. We need to find a solution to this vexing situation.*

Yours from Barter's Hill, half-way up or half-way down, take your pick,

Aaron.

Next thing Meta Maud did was to pick up an ordinary pen and she wrote a letter. She started it off to herself. *Dear Meta Maud*, it said, and she wrote it pretty fast. She was good with words, she was smart that way. All the Grandys had brains, even Clyde had brains. For Clyde they didn't fire off right, yet, but she knew they would. When she finished, she phoned up Eunice Cluett.

"How's Aaron? He's not dying anymore, he's oxygenated again? That's good, let me speak to him."

"This is Aaron Stoodley."

"Aaron?"

"Meta Maud. It's you."

"Aaron, I'm sending you a letter at last, but it's to me."

"To you?"

"To me."

"I don't get it. That makes no sense."

"You'll see. What you do is this. When you get my letter, copy it out in your own handwriting. Each line exactly the same, even the start of each line the same. Exactly, but in your hand. Then you mail it back to me the same day. End it up with this: *Your lover, Aaron Stoodley*. You got it?"

"Your lover? Did I hear you say that, Meta Maud?"

"That's what we're going to write."

"Your lover. I'm not your lover."

"Just copy it out and send it back, the same day."

Then Meta Maud Grandy went downstairs into the basement and put the letters and the magazines back into the diving bag. She found her suitcase and took it upstairs and packed up everything she had and called a cab. Then she phoned up her old friend from school, Germaine, and she said, "Germaine, I'm staying with you a few days?" and Germaine said, "Sure." She didn't ask why.

Then Meta Maud Grandy walked out on Harold Butts and never left a note. Nothing.

Three days later, Harold Butts still couldn't figure it out. He'd come home after a real fine day and she was gone. Like she was never there, ever, and the condo was back just the way he had it before. The first thing he did, he went down into the basement and there were the letters and the magazines, still in the bag. She never found them then, that was good. The next day, he phoned in sick for the first time in ten years. To hell with them, he had plenty of sick pay coming. "Touch of the flu," he said. "You sure? We're shorthanded." "Try throwing up in your regulator, that's no fun." "Okay, Harold, see you when you're better." He was the best man they had there underwater, he knew that, he could do whatever he liked. Then he sat there for three days staring at the walls and the mailman came by and dropped a letter in the box. When he picked the letter up, it was for her, from that same loser. To hell with the kettle, he ripped the letter open with his fingers.

The letter said,

> *Dear Meta Maud, how fine to hear*
> *a voice that's*
> *really you on the phone, the*
> *lovely times we had*
> *in English Harbour, the*
> *night sky, the lightning bugs, the*
> *ghosts in the shadows, the walks on*
> *Gower Street and Barter's Hill*
> *I'm the man for you*
> *remember me the way it was. Your*
> *lover, Aaron Stoodley.*

He took out his purple pen and circled the first letter of each line.

Darling girl.

She knew Harold Butts'd figure it out. He'd get the bends from it, the sweetness sliding through him in the kitchen. It was the last thing he'd ever steal from her, this letter.

She felt strong, like now she was the one breathing pure oxygen.

clothes-pin

I KNOW YOU'LL never think of me again but as this shy boy, smitten, a mote, brush-me-away as ordinary as a picket fence, as long grass, and you can easily forget the wedding where, by forced circumstance, you danced with me, incongruous, our ages risible; I was nothing but a clothespin on your dress, a dragonfly, harmless and ornamental, as inconspicuous then as now, when, within another crowd, you take your last walk down to the boat bound for Halifax, your body angulated by the suitcase, hand-me-down, your new shoes dusted up in gravel, your last wave dispensed to all, and the small boats in the harbour, disused, orchestrated now by a shimmer of breeze, swing upon their tethers, and the canted hills bend seaward, bruised, protective, so concerned to see you go.

the eye

CYRIL SAVOURY WAS born with one weak eye. It was the left one and it wandered out the same way, to the left, drifting.

"What a fine baby," they all said. "But what about that eye, Rosetta, what's that about?"

In answer to that particular question, Rosetta said, "Well, I guess that's just Cyril's eye, that's the way it is."

No one could comment with any certainty on the genetic contribution—to the wandering eye—made by Cyril's father, because he'd only been in town once, for two weeks, and then he was mysteriously gone.

"I remember," said somebody, "he had brown hair, didn't he?"

"I don't remember," said somebody else, "but this baby of Rosetta's, he's either got dark hair or he's bald."

Rosetta was out of the room when they were talking.

"Rub your hand on there," one of them said, "on top of his little head, you'll feel frizz—watch out for the soft spot—but look, there's some dark hair down there, on the nape of his neck. Five fingers, five toes, everything else you need."

Then Rosetta came back into the room and they said, "Too bad about the eye, Rosetta, but it doesn't matter because otherwise, but for the one eye, that's some cute baby."

When she put on the knitted baby hat, the thrum cap—the one she got from her aunt—when she put it on Cyril, it made his eye look worse. How could that be?

She took the cap off and she held him up by the armpits like all her relatives did, like they did with all babies, and she turned him this way and that, and spun him around, and he really looked fine—especially if she turned him just far enough that she could see only one of his eyes at a time. Then he was perfect. But when she tied Cyril's new hat back on, using the strings provided, the weak eye jumped out at her like an arrow to the heart. His eyes, the hat, they were the same blue colour. Maybe that was it, they reflected back upon each other, magnifying the problem. Forget wearing hats at all, she figured. So she let him go through the early months bare-headed, unless they went outside in the bitter cold.

Tell the truth, she was a bit torn up by the eye. There was a tight feeling in her throat that came and went of its own accord. Everybody wants everything perfect all the time, and I guess I'm like that, she thought. Then, when he was ten weeks old and he started to smile with pleasure, and gurgle and laugh, she almost forgot about the eye. She didn't look at it, or it became such an accustomed part of what she saw, day in and day out, that she hardly noticed it anymore, when they were alone. But everybody else noticed it.

"Kootchee-kootchee-koo," they said to Cyril, chuckling him under the chin, but as they chuckled, they looked at his eye and wondered how Cyril would do in life, how he'd get along with an eye like that, one that wandered out into left field with a mind of its own.

They took him to St. John's to see the specialist. To do that, they had to take the coastal boat and then the taxi from Terrenceville. Her mother and father came along for the ride to help her out, the three of them together with the little bundle that was Cyril. They took turns holding him, and, for a baby, he seemed to like the trip. He looked around in his own fashion. He was easy-going all the time, and, naturally, they wondered what he saw.

"Maybe he sees as much as we do," Rosetta said, "maybe even twice as much."

"Maybe he sees less," said her father, "or the same amount as we do, but blurred. You know, if you leave the eye like that, it goes blind."

"Don't say that," said Rosetta's mother, "that's why we're here in this taxi. Rosetta, let me hold the baby now."

They stayed overnight in a rooming-house downtown, and early the next morning they went to the doctor's office. All three of them got to go in with the baby.

"Hi there, Cyril Savoury," said the doctor, but then he introduced himself to Rosetta and her parents and shook their hands, one by one, looking at each one of them directly in the eye. As though that was part of his examination. To Rosetta, he looked to be as old as her grandfather. That's good, she thought, here's a doctor who in his lifetime has seen a lot, so he'll know what to do.

"Put the baby down there, on the examining table," he said.

Then the doctor left the room and a nurse put drops in Cyril's eyes and Cyril cried for five or ten seconds and the nurse said, "Let's wait fifteen minutes now, so those eyedrops, they have time to work, okay?"

"Okay," they all said at once, all three of them.

They waited and finally the doctor came back and loomed over the baby with his light. Cyril squirmed away but didn't say anything, or cry anymore, even though the old doctor was bent over close enough that their cheeks touched. Then the doctor wiggled his fingers in front of Cyril's face. He picked the baby up and rotated him back and forth, just like Rosetta had done when he was wearing the blue thrum cap. Then he gave him back to Rosetta.

"That's a well-behaved little boy you got there, you're doing something right, with this boy."

"Well," said Rosetta's mother, "thank you, he is a good boy, but what about the eye?"

"There should be no surgery for an eye like this," the doctor said, "not at this age. You could do a lot more harm than good. The best thing for him, for this boy, is the patch, the pirate's patch."

"The pirate's patch?" Rosetta asked, "what's that?"

"It's a shaped piece of dark cloth, that's all. We cover up the right eye, the good one, with it. It's black, it blocks out the light. You leave the patch on, Miss Savoury, over the good eye, half the day every day, and during that time the left eye, the lazy eye, it's on its own, it's forced to do all the work. It tracks you round the room, it sees the trees, the birds, the spoon, the bottle. That way, it learns to see on its own and it does not go blind."

"Oh Doctor," Rosetta's mother said, "that's such good news."

Rosetta's mother had tears rolling down her cheeks, as though she were alone in the room, as though she had no shame at all, to be displaying such emotion in front of strangers.

"Where do we get the patches from?" Rosetta asked the nurse, after the doctor shook their hands again, formally, and bowed and left the room.

"Why, we'll give you some, we got lots and lots."

She went over to a drawer and opened it and inside were hundreds of little black patches stacked into each other, like Dixie cups.

"Here's one that should fit Cyril," she said.

She put the patch, shaped like an oval, over Cyril's right eye. There was a black elastic band connected to it that she looped over his forehead and then over the back of his head.

"It's easier to do," she said, "once he's got more hair, because the elastic kind of sticks better then, you'll see."

"How long do we keep this up?" Rosetta asked.

"Till his eye goes straight, or till he's six."

"Six months?"

"No, six years my dear, six years. That's how it works, it's a long haul."

Well, they figured, that left lots of time for the eye to get better on its own, six years ticking by. It would seem like forever but it wouldn't be that long, in the grand scheme of things.

After they left the office, Rosetta said, "Did you see all those patches? There must be hundreds of kids like Cyril."

"Oh, I don't think so," said Rosetta's mother, "you and I know there's nobody quite like Cyril."

"I'll say," said her father, laughing to himself, waving down a taxi for them.

On the way home, they kept the patch on more than half the time. Everybody who bent over him, in the taxi, on the wharf, and on the boat, looked at him and smiled and said, well, there's a cute little boy. Must be some kind of pirate, your baby, look at him, how about that! They went on and on about Cyril, and Rosetta was happy now because he was well on the way to being the perfect boy she always knew he was.

Despite the patch though—which every morning she applied and left on until the middle of the afternoon—Cyril's eye never seemed to focus like it should. Months went by and it still lay askew, and Rosetta was disappointed. She phoned up the nurse in St. John's for advice, as she'd been told to do.

"Keep putting on the corrective patch, dear. You have to have the necessary patience, and persistence, Miss Savoury. The brain and the lazy eye need to recalibrate, and it takes a long long time."

That's what she heard every time she phoned.

"Stay the course, Miss Savoury."

She began to have dreams in which it was nighttime and she went to pick the sleeping baby up from the crib, and there he was with both eyes now covered up in black. Oh my God. She reached for him and touched him and he opened his mouth to cry, like babies do at night, and out flew a string of those patches. They were like bats coming right at her. She woke up, startled, jumped up out of bed and ran over to the crib by the window. Now she was wide-awake, her heart was thumping, and moonlight came through the lace curtains and washed down over Cyril and carried on through the slats in the crib, leaving a pattern on the floor. Of course there were no patches on his eyes. No bats. It was just another dream, yet so real. Cyril was fine. He always had his right arm up and out, with a fist, when he slept. He never woke up. She was blessed with that, how he slept so peacefully.

She got out all the old photographs of the family and sat down with her mother. "Let's look for the lazy eye, where it came from," she said.

One by one they went through a box half-full of dog-eared snapshots, the old black-and-whites they'd put away upstairs, all taken by the same Brownie camera. Actually, there were some older ones too, larger sized, but where they came from, they were uncertain. There were a lot of group shots, mostly from weddings, but all that Rosetta and her mother looked at were the eyes.

"There," they said, "that girl looks as if her right eye's gone adrift. Check her out in the other pictures. Who is she anyway?"

"I can't remember, I'm trying to place her."

"Give me some of them, Mother, let me help."

They sifted through all the pictures to find another one of the same girl. There she was, there she was this time standing on the shore with a boat pulled up behind her. She was older then, and her eyes this time were as straight as a ruler.

"Look, she got better. Maybe that first picture, maybe it was just the angle?"

"Hard to tell, hard to tell."

They wondered once again what Cyril actually saw when his eye rolled out in the way it did. He sure seemed smart enough.

When Rosetta brought him the baby bottle, he reached for it with both hands, babbling away, and at the same time, with his left eye, he could watch a gull swing by the window. They could see him follow it with a quick flick, like a pulse.

Finally, on day three of their investigation, they found a picture of someone, way back in olden times, sitting in a parlour, posed. He had on a suit and a tie and there was a picture on the wall, over his shoulder, of a ship under sail. His left eye was just like Cyril's, turned out and away. There was no doubt about it, this time.

"Who's that, Mother?"

"Again, I have no idea. I'm sorry. Look, there's our family clock though, so he must be a relation."

"These days," said Rosetta, "they'd retouch this photograph and fix that eye."

Her mother said that sure, they could retouch things now, like blemishes, but it was impossible back then, because in those days you had to hold still for pictures, it took such a long time for daylight to fix on old-fashioned film, if you moved even one iota during the exposure, it would blur. So maybe this man, their relative, moved his eyes.

"Then both eyes would look crooked, the same," pointed out Rosetta.

"You had to stand as motionless as an Egyptian Sphinx," her mother said, "but you're right, if that was the case, both his eyes would be off."

No one they consulted had the slightest idea who the man was, but they went and pinned up his photo in the kitchen anyway. That way, they figured, Cyril had someone to relate to, if his eye stayed that way despite the patch, despite all the prayers they made at night, despite the hopes that never deserted them, despite the way he learned to walk with a little stagger, half the time looking, through no fault of his own, like a bandit. Or like a shirt salesman, they soon found out. There was a man who posed with shirts in the magazines, always dressed up to the nines. He wore a black patch too. They put his picture, once they found it, in Cyril's bedroom. They scotch-taped it onto the mirror on the dresser, and it was still there twenty-five years later, yellowed and crumpled and torn at the edges, in that room that had been empty for such a long time.

The best the eye ever got was when he was about three or four. At that time, he was always in the company of his mother or his grandmother, or more likely both.

"The patch, Cyril," they always said, "be a good boy, put on the patch, train that eye."

There was no way they'd let him slack off and leave the patch at home. So that was the time—if ever a time ever was—for the lazy eye to straighten out and do the right thing. But after that, after four years old, no matter how hard they tried, it seemed that Cyril's eye developed a mind of its own. It stayed where it wanted to be. On top of that, the few times that Cyril wandered down the road by himself, when he was a toddler, he pulled the patch off. He'd drop it on the side of the road, on purpose, or in the long grass, as if by accident. But it seemed that each and every one of those patches had nine lives.

"Hey, look what I found, here's Cyril's black eye patch," some boy or girl would say, standing excitedly by the door, holding it up.

"We found it up the road," they'd say.

Or, several times, the dog came home with it in his mouth.

"Cyril," Rosetta would say, "please don't do that, your patch is the best chance we got."

When he was six, back they went to the same eye specialist. They got on the boat and then into the taxi and all the way to town. The doctor looked even older and he had a shake in his right hand when he bent over Cyril with the light.

"Don't mind the little shake," the doctor said, "I can still see fine. You know, I'm sorry to say, but this boy's eye has not improved a whit, it's time for surgery."

Rosetta said, "But what can go wrong with surgery, Doctor? We kind of like Cyril the way he is, really, he seems to get around okay."

"Well," said the doctor, "that's a good question, the main trouble with the surgery is that if we over-correct the weak eye, then Cyril's eye will point inwards and sit by the nose. It's like shortening the leg on a kitchen table, you can overdo it."

"That's bad," said Rosetta.

"That would be worse than now," said Rosetta's mother.

"He'd look goofy then," said her father.

They all imagined the crossed eye, sitting by the nose.

"Why sure, Cyril then, he'd look foolish," said Rosetta.

"Well yes," said the doctor, "that's sort of true, but then there can be further surgery to correct the surgery. We usually get it right at some point."

"You mean," asked Rosetta's mother, "there'd be surgery to correct the surgery that corrected the old surgery?"

"That has happened, yes, but more in the old days," said the doctor, "when it was more an inexact science than it is now."

"That won't do for Cyril," said Rosetta.

She and her parents didn't sign up for the operation after all. They took Cyril home and took off his eye patch.

"Cyril," they said, "just go out and play."

After that, they gave up on any treatment. They all just accepted the eye for what it was. Cyril went off to school like everyone else, but it turned out that the eye was not the only thing gone wrong. No matter what Cyril did, he couldn't seem to learn to read at all. It was like there was a space missing in his brain, or as if part of his brain was following that wayward eye, wandering off on its own and not paying attention. This caused problems for Cyril. Everybody knew he was smart. He could remember anything, and draw things with a pencil and a pen that came out looking like life, even when he was just eight years old.

The trouble was, because he couldn't read, the school failed him year after year, no matter what Albert May, the teacher, thought and wanted to do. Albert May had no choice. The rules for the school district were rigid and could not, apparently, be bent. He wrote the District Superintendent annually for four years, begging him to come out and see Cyril, to talk to him. You'll see, he wrote, he's way too smart to hold back because of some generalization, some standard rule.

After a long while that spoke of indifference, the District Supervisor relented and came out and talked directly to Cyril. He agreed with Albert May.

"This boy is very intelligent, that's for sure, you're right, but, Mr. May, he's handicapped not only by his appearance, he's not reading and the rules are plain: we have to hold him back."

The teacher protested, saying the rules would destroy the boy, that there was an exception for every rule.

"Not in my district," the man said, closing the door to his car, "it's a shitkicker but if he can't read books, he can't move on, end of story."

"Wait," said Albert May, "I'll quit if you make me fail that boy again."

He was bending down into the car, holding onto the mirror and the half-closed window.

"So be it," said the District Supervisor, "go ahead and quit, all the reports I got on you aren't the best anyway, there's others that would come out here, believe it or not, there's unemployment in our noble profession."

He drove away and went back to Grand Falls.

Albert May added up the pros and cons and figured out that both he and Cyril Savoury would be better off if he didn't quit, if he stayed. He actually liked the job, and what else could he do? Also, there was his mother to support.

So he took matters into his own hands and he wrote down FAILED, in black capital letters, like he was supposed to, on Cyril's report card. He sent that one, the official report, to the district. But when he wrote down the word FAILED he inserted a thin piece of cardboard under the top page of the form, so the word did not pass through onto the carbon paper, to the copies beneath. On those copies, which stayed in town, he wrote PASSED, and that was the copy that went home that year, with Cyril, to his mother. And the next year, and the next year the same. He told no one what he had done.

On the reports, he also wrote things like: *Cyril is a smart boy who participates well in class. Though he cannot read at this time, he is learning to script his name. His spoken work and his contribution to class is exemplary. If every boy in this class were as accomplished as Cyril, my job as a teacher would be even more wonderful than it is now.*

Rosetta and her mother and Cyril rejoiced over his progress and his advancement and they danced around the kitchen. And their dance was not in vain, for when the time came for Cyril to graduate from primary school, three years later, the old District Superintendant was gone, promoted to Cornerbrook. He was replaced by a young woman and the young woman came uninvited down the gravel road in a small car with dust flying out behind her. She had a sheaf of FAILEDs in her hand, to see for herself this hopeless boy who broke all the records for ineptitude.

"Where is he?" she asked Albert May.

"He's in there, but first here's the real reports, the ones he really got, the ones I gave him and his mother."

Albert May handed over the evidence of his years of deceit.

She read them all, looked at Albert May, and then she walked into the classroom where Cyril sat all by himself. After ten minutes, the new District Superintendent came back out.

"Mr. May, in my opinion, you showed real good judgment

when you broke the rules. Move this boy on. You know, he looks good too, once you get used to the eye."

"We don't even see that eye anymore," said Mr. May, "it doesn't register upon us."

She drove back up the road, and must have fixed up the old reports in the District Office because Cyril had no further troubles in school again, even though he never really learned to read letters at all. He did all his learning within his head, and he had just the one teacher all the way along, Albert May.

The night she got pregnant with Cyril, Rosetta had on a little dress that wasn't much more than a shift. It was the hottest time of summer. She went walking with the boy with wavy hair, up the road, and then down the hill to Back Cove. They could swim there if the blackflies weren't too bad. Rosetta didn't even realize what had happened to her till it was over. She didn't have a clue. The only way she could hide was to press in closer to him, to squeeze up to him so he couldn't see her. It was the only place she could go. Thinking back, she didn't think he had a lazy eye, that boy, but she couldn't remember with certainty. What did she know about him? Nothing. She never saw him when he was tired, when the sun shone down enough to make him squint, or when he was sick with a fever of 101 degrees. Maybe, at times like those, maybe his eye wandered off like Cyril's did. Yes, after Back Cove, it was hard for Rosetta, the worst of times. She grew bigger and all the eyes in the world stared straight at her, watching her. Then Cyril came along and she was left alone with that lovely little patched-up baby, by herself, only her own mother and father there to help.

"You little pirate," she said to him before they gave up the patch for good, "you little pirate, whatever are we going to do with you?"

burin

CYRIL SAVOURY'S FIRST job, after he left school, was in St. John's, at the Arts and Culture Centre, where his uncle William secured for him a temporary position as a security guard, with a grey uniform that fit him perfectly, a brown leather belt, a walkie-talkie, and a hat with such a military cast that Cyril stopped at his reflection in the lobby glass; it was in this uniform that Cyril presented himself for work on October 14th, for a show on loan from the German National Museum, featuring twenty prints by Albrecht Dürer, and although he had no knowledge of the underlying themes of Dürer's work, Cyril found himself, on the very first morning of his employment, mesmerized, carefully examining the cross-hatching—the fine parallel and intersecting lines of shading—on the thigh of a horse in the engraving *Knight, Death, and Devil*; after lunch the gallery was full, for the show had been praised in the *Evening Telegram* and in the *Daily News*, and Cyril felt himself being drawn back through the crowds to the same work, where the cross-hatching was so dense, so varied, so thick here and so thin there, so magnificently cross-hatched everywhere that he did not see, developing around him, within the web of his security, the shambles of a public gallery left without any supervision at all: there was a young man standing so close to *Melencolia* that he could breathe upon it, a boy from Bay Roberts touching the frame of *St. Eustache*, and young men smirking in front of *Adam and Eve*—Cyril saw none of this, he saw only that he was tapped on the shoulder by the Chief of Security, that he was terminated for cause that very afternoon, that he lost his uniform, his belt, his walkie-talkie, and the military hat but, somehow, he had not lost his self-esteem, for with the few dollars he was given for his labours, he bought that day on Duckworth Street a set of pencils and a hand-sharpener, and in the evening he drew, hesitatingly at first but then with confidence, a true likeness of his own hand and sleeve, and the next day he woke up early and drew, from memory, the laundry on Hilda Cluett's line, with the northeast wind snapping at the cotton sheets like a lost opportunity, and he drew the rockface Iron Skull and the Burin shore, and he cross-hatched it, as Albrecht Dürer would have done, had he been Cyril Savoury.

rigor mortis

"HE'S DEAD."

"He's what?"

"He's dead. He's out there lying by the fire."

"Dead? Ralph?"

"Get up. Come see, double-check. Bring the mirror."

"The mirror?"

"Bring the shaving kit, it's got the mirror."

They both crawled out of the tent. The sun was just up. The air was fresh and there was Ralph, lying on his side, stretched out by the ashes of the fire, still in the clothes he had on when he went to bed last night. He had brought his own little pup tent to sleep in, separate from theirs.

"Oh look at him, I think you're right."

"Give me the mirror."

"Here."

"We'll check."

"Check what?"

"For the spark of life. Hold it over the lips, real close like this."

"He's alive! There's a smudge on the glass!"

"That's your fingerprint."

"You think?"

"Look at the whorls! Give me that hankie."

They rubbed the mirror carefully with one corner of the handkerchief until the mirror was perfect. The red of the rising sun reflected off it, and the light flickered over Ralph's face too, and then along the ground until it disappeared into the bushes. Ralph's eyes were stuck open.

"Eyes look dry."

"That's the stare of death."

"Ralph!"

"Ralph!"

"Push him a bit, on the shoulder. See what happens."

"Like this?"

"Like that but a little bit more. Harder."

"There. Oh Christ lookout!"

Ralph toppled right over onto the flat of his back. They were camped, the three of them, by the side of the Skeena River which flowed by, smooth and silent for a river of that size. There were mountains in the distance and, close-up, there were trees, lots of evergreen trees that grew up by the campsite. You could see the ashes of a fire.

"Hey, go blow on those embers."

"The embers?"

"It's coffee time."

"Coffee now?"

"Regardless."

"Okay. Back off, I'll blow on the embers."

"Harder than that. Briskly."

"I'm dizzy. Oh, there we go."

"Good."

"There, how's that?"

"Now fire, that's the real spark of life. Without fire, there's no civilization."

"Here's the mirror, try again."

"Okay."

"Hold it closer, maybe he's breathing wispy."

"Wispy?"

"Real low. I saw it on TV."

"There."

"You touched the lips."

"I did? I did not."

"Maybe. Anyway, there's nothing there. Nothing."

"He's gone. Gone for good."

"You're right. The mirror doesn't lie."

Birds flew about the campsite every morning. They were mostly grey jays and they flew real close, trying to pick up little crumbs with their beaks. There was some kind of sparrow too, jumping around in the low bushes. You could tell it was going to be a fine day, but it was still cool. They were glad they had on their checked red-and-black wool jackets.

"You know, this is now some pickle we're in."

"Just the two of us."

"That's right. Just us. It's just kind of hitting me."

"Long way to go?"

"I'll say. Three hundred miles, from the map."

"Portages?"

"Three."

"Big ones, little ones?"

"Two are big."

"Uphill?"

"Uphill."

"Jeez."

Then there was one of those silences you sometimes get in

nature. The river spun against the rocks on the shoreline but for some reason it didn't make a sound.

"Better check him out for animal bites."

"Animal bites? What do you mean?"

"Well, maybe he didn't just die on his own, maybe he got killed."

"Killed? How could that happen?"

"A cougar, one of those grizzly bears."

"The ones we saw upriver? They were eating fish."

"At that time they were eating fish."

"I guess, that size, they eat a lot."

"They eat fish, they eat berries, they eat meat. They are carnivores. In fact, they are the world's largest carnivore, after the polar bear."

"There's no polar bears here. Right?"

"No. At least I hope not. They are merciless killers, polar bears, relentless in their pursuit of meat. They will track a human being a hundred miles."

"They like seals better. That's what I heard."

"Ralph. You think he looks like a seal?"

Ralph's pack, the grey one, was right there by the closed flap of his pup tent. Everything looked in perfect order. The stones around the fire formed a circle.

"Not really like a seal, no. But then I've never seen a seal. They got soft pads on their feet, grizzly bears, polar bears."

"I heard nothing all night. Did you?"

"No, nothing. Not a peep."

"They can walk on twigs, soundless as a ghost."

"A Wendigo."

"Oh, don't say that, that gives me the chills."

"Big cats now, they bite you in the back of the neck, right?"

"Definitely. They are sneaky. Bears on the other hand, they

come right at you, they have fetid breath, they knock you down with their paws. Then they chew your head."

A red canoe was pulled up on the rocks by the river and there were three paddles leaning on a tree. There was no sign of a violent struggle. The forest floor was smooth with pine needles.

"Let's look for blood."

"You mean inside the clothes?"

"First close his eyes. I don't like that stare, that unseeing stare. It gives me the willies."

"Ralph's eyes?"

"Yes, Ralph's eyes."

"Touch them?"

"The eyelids, that's all. Use your fingertips."

"I blew on the fire. I rolled him over. You close the eyes."

"Okay, I guess that's fair. You got that hankie?"

"Hankie's no good. Just use your fingertips, like you said."

"Fingertips."

"There. That's it. Push down, be firm. Hold them there for a bit. Good. Now let go."

"They're half-open again."

"Let's push him over. Then we don't have to look. Push him away from the fire."

"Altogether now 1-2-3…"

"Go!"

"Heavy."

"Heavier dead than alive. That's why they say dead weight."

When they pushed him over, there was no sign of damage to the back of Ralph's head. All he had there was a few red welts from mosquito bites, and deer flies. They all had lots of those.

"No blood, no bites."

"Well, that's a relief."

"I'll say."

"Killer bear, that's the last thing we need on this trip."

"I think we got freaked out over nothing. Heart attack, that's my guess."

"This trip, I thought we planned it real well."

Seven months before the trip had started, they each had a list to go over. They checked off all the clothes they needed, the pills they might need. They were careful in every way, right down to the salt and pepper. They even went to the doctor and had checkups.

"Hey, what about CPR?"

"CPR?"

"You know, mouth-to-mouth resuscitation?"

"For Ralph? Here?"

"Of course for Ralph, look at him, he's the one that needs it."

"We rolled him over the wrong way for that."

"I'm not skilled in that, CPR. I couldn't do it."

"You hold their nose, you breathe into their mouth."

"You know how, you try it. We should do it."

"We?"

"You. You know how. Here, I'll flip him back. There. Give it a go."

"He's got a cold sore."

"Where?"

"There on the upper lip."

"This? It's all crusted."

"That's it though."

"They're catching aren't they, cold sores? They're viruses?"

"Damn right they are."

"Then there's no CPR for Ralph. Besides, he's not fresh enough."

"What do you mean?"

"Dead too long. It's hopeless. Look, whatever killed Ralph, it happened in the night. His fingers are stiff."

"That's normal, stiffening, right?"

"Right, but not if you're freshly dead. Then, fresh, your fingers are still loose, supple like ours."

"CPR is hopeless then for Ralph, now."

"Right."

"No CPR then. Forget it. I don't like the look of that cold sore."

"Then what are we going to say to Phyllis? He died and we did nothing for him?"

Ralph had been married for forty years. He was a retired pharmacist with grown-up children. They'd known his wife, Phyllis, forever. They played bridge together, and Scrabble.

"There's nothing we could do. Nothing useful."

"Maybe we can make up this part, what do you think?"

"You mean, how we did CPR?"

"That's right."

"Two hours non-stop, for Ralph."

"We took turns."

"We pushed on his chest."

"Till God knows we could push no more."

"Slapped his face?"

"That too."

"Shouted out Ralph, Ralph, over and over."

"We actually did that, the shouting. Remember?"

"That's right. It's not all made up."

"No, we did that all right."

"That's good then. That's the story."

"That's what friends do for friends. CPR."

"Even, Phyllis, with the cold sore he had. We didn't care."

"How many hours?"

"Two hours, I'd say. Felt like six."

"I'll say. It feels like that already."

They'd been on the canoe trip for twelve days, and they had another three days to go. Resigned, they left Ralph where he was and made some coffee. They fried up back-bacon too, and the smoke from the frying pan curled around the clearing. As yet, there was no wind.

"I guess we don't have to scrimp and save quite so much."

"How do you mean?"

"The bacon. Only two of us now, but there's food for three. It's the silver lining." "Oh, the silver lining. Sure, I see. Another slice then please, my stomach is growling. It's been a tough morning. Thank you, Ralph, old friend."

"That's good?"

"Better than good. Crispy."

"Mine too. Now what are we going to do?"

"With Ralph?"

"That's the first question."

"I say bury him. Bury him right here like they would in the old days."

There was sand and pebbles on the ground but it was all packed tight. Digging through that would not be easy. There'd be roots from trees.

"This is where he'd like to be, I bet. Out in nature."

"Oh I don't think so."

"He loved the north."

"He also loved the easy chair, the Laz-Y-Boy."

"Well that's true, I grant you that."

"It's against the law, burying. We can't dispose of Ralph right off, bury him without some sort of official check."

"We could be charged with murder. You're right. I just thought of it."

"Murder?"

NICHOLAS RUDDOCK

"They could say we banged him on the head with paddles, we smothered him with a life jacket, then we buried him. We'd be old men by the time we got out."

"We didn't kill Ralph."

"Prove it, with Ralph buried here."

"We'd come back with the police, dig him up."

"If we're going to do that, then let's not bury him now in the first place. Digging with spoons, that's no fun."

"I see what you mean."

"He comes with us, Ralph does, that's all there is to it."

"The grizzlies, they'd dig him up too, if we left him here."

"Probably, and where's the evidence then of our innocence, our CPR? He's got to come with us. All the way home."

You had to have resources to travel in the north. You had to adjust. You needed a compass, a watch, skills with rope, strong legs for portages, and courage for the wild animals you saw along the way. You could not get knocked down by bad luck, you had to overcome everything thrown your way.

"Well, how do we pack him up?"

"He goes in the canoe with all the rest."

"With the baggage."

"That's it, baggage. That's what Ralph is now."

"He's getting stiffer."

"In the fingers?"

"Everywhere. Soon he'll be stiff as a board. Feel him."

"That's what nature does. Rigor mortis, that's what it's called."

"Rigor mortis. I heard of that."

"Latin. Stiffness of death, something like that. It means we got some thinking to do. Quick thinking."

"I don't see the rush."

"You don't? Think about it."

Up till now, all three of them had paddled the same canoe at the same time, with Ralph in the middle. Compared to the others, Ralph was inexperienced. He did not have the stamina for long hours on the river, nor the skill for the bow or the stern. He made up for this deficiency by singing songs.

"Yes, think about it. There's Ralph. Straight out the way he is, he'll be like that soon, forever. Frozen up stiff as a board. Next portage, a straight uphill for five miles, what are we going to do with Ralph like that? Carry him, the two of us, like he's a plank? No thanks, that's what I say."

"Drag him on saplings. Tie him on, drag him the way the Indians did."

"They knew how to do that. We don't. Also, they had horses."

"We could try."

"Sure, we could try. And you know what? There goes Ralph slipping down the trail and over a cliff. Tumbling through the air, I can see it plain as day. Then he's at the bottom, food for the weasels and wolves and then the Mounties say, well fellows, where's your friend Ralph, the one you beat over the head with paddles, where's he now?"

"That does not sound good."

"We need another plan. Before the rigor mortis sets in, we put Ralph into a better shape."

"What do mean by that? You lost me there."

"The river's no problem. He can be in any position for the river. Plank shape, it doesn't matter. But for the portages, stiff as a board, forget it, that's impossible. We'd have to make two, even three trips. One just for him alone. No way."

"So what should we do?"

"Bend him. Turn him into a shape like a back-pack. Look, he's got some give left in him still. We can twist him this way, that way, anyway we like, but not for long. Then, we get him into the right position, we hold him there so he freezes like that. Simple.

Twenty minutes, half an hour."

They went over to where Ralph was lying. They grabbed his coat and bent him at the waist, so he sat up at ninety degrees, and then they took his arms and raised them up to the height of his shoulders. Then they bent his elbows, and they pushed and pulled at his wrists and his fingers till they turned into claw shapes.

"Look. He's got talons now, like an eagle."

Then they hiked up Ralph's hips and bent them outwards, and they held Ralph in that position for a half-hour or more while the grey jays flew by and the sun rose ever higher in the sky.

"There. We can let him go now. Try it."

"That's good. Look! It worked."

"Perfect, I agree. He's fixed like this forever. Now, try him on."

"Try him on?"

"Like a back-pack. That was the whole purpose of the exercise."

"You try him on."

"I closed the eyelids, right? It's your turn. Try him on. Next portage, it's the canoe and the rifle for me, and there's Ralph for you. Up on your back, easy as pie, one-man job. Then, there's no getting around it, we both make a second trip for all the rest of the gear."

"For me, that's not so good."

"Why's that?"

"Well first off, there's Ralph breathing down my neck on the portage, plus the fact he weighs one hundred eighty pounds."

"He's balanced, he's easy to move along with. Try him on. And there's no way he's breathing down your neck. He's dead. The dead don't breathe."

"The canoe weighs fifty-two pounds."

"Okay, we'll take turns with Ralph, how's that, that's fair."

"That's a deal."

"You do the first turn, I'll do the second."

"Okay. Boost him up, I'll give him a try. We can't stay here forever."

"There."

"Hey that's not too bad. What about the hands?"

"Tie them across your chest. Like this. How's that feel? Solid?"

"Well, he's no featherweight."

"But you can do it."

"I think I can. How far off my neck is that cold sore?"

"Lots of room there. An inch. Funny thing, from behind, I can't see your head at all. Just his. Looks funny."

"Take him off, that's enough for now. Stop laughing."

They broke camp. All the gear was carefully stowed away in the middle of the canoe, and on top of the gear, they placed Ralph's body, firmly tied onto the very top, on his back, with his legs and arms sticking up skyward. He looked like the rack of a deer, so stiff he was, with the rigor mortis set in solid. Nothing could move those arms and legs. They grabbed their paddles and they pushed off into the current.

"Tally-ho!"

It felt good to be back on the river. Cleansing, after what they'd been through. They slipped and danced through the easy small rapids and they made good time.

"Hold on tight there, Ralph!"

Now and then they rubbed the canoe on a low boulder but they slid on by, harmlessly.

"Don't shift your weight like that, Ralph!" they laughed, "That's a good boy! Hold on there, just twelve miles to the next portage! Tally-ho!"

Unknown to the canoeists, on that next portage, three miles up the steep and brambled path, sunning itself on a rock, was a large male cougar. This cougar was four years old, and in those four years, there was nothing this cougar had not killed, dragged and swallowed whole, so big and powerful he was. Now, the cougar felt a pang of hunger, and he yawned, and moved his massive limbs into a more comfortable position. There was still time to wait, he thought, for what might come by. No need to start prowling around.

Indeed, four hours later, he heard a racket. He drew back from his sunny rock. There was a big canoe coming up the hill, and now and then it would sway and bang into trees. There were human legs underneath that red shell, promising enough for a meal, but maybe a bit too much work? Yawn some more, that's what the cougar did, but he shifted his weight again, now onto his hind legs. What's that coming next? This was getting interesting. This had to be the biggest, thickest human being he'd ever seen. He could hear heavy breathing, a lingering funny odour wafting his way. Now's the time. The hiker walked on by, slowly, staggering up the steep rise of the hill, as though sick, so slow, and then it was, with padded feet and teeth like spikes, that the big cougar slipped down from the sunny rock onto the path, and silently gained speed until he hit poor Ralph, the backpack, so hard on the back of the neck that he snapped Ralph's spine in four places. Down went the hiker, pine needles in the face.

The funny thing was, the cougar thought, this piece of meat kept on shouting and shouting no matter how many times he shook the neck, no matter how many times he broke the spine, no matter how he twisted his victim's head around and around again until he could see the whole face.

What's that? Bang, bang, two bullets whipped by the cougar's ears.

He gave up and ran from the spectre of his victim, from the man who stared up at him with his eyes all now open, a scab on the upper lip, the smell of death already upon him.

Ten days later, to his chagrin, the cougar developed a nasty sore on his right upper lip, just above the incisor. Every time he snarled, it hurt. That painful sore, that little ulcer seemed to come back forever, over and over again for the next fifteen years. It served as a cruel reminder, to the cougar, of that big mistake he made, back there by the sunny rock. After that, he left all human beings alone. He stuck to elk and grouse and rabbits.

When they finally got home, Ralph's two canoeing buddies told the whole story to everybody they met. In their excitement, they almost forgot about the hours of CPR they performed down by the river. Then they remembered it, and they got a plaque from the Red Cross. They told everyone how lucky they were, how Ralph had saved their lives when the cougar struck, how he'd stepped in when he was needed, even though he was dead. Their poor friend was buried soon after they got home, buried like the hero he was. Unfortunately, he was unfit for an open casket.

The funeral director said, "No, Phyllis, I am sorry but there is no way, despite my schooling, despite my many, many years of experience, there is no way I can fix up Ralph, as you remember him, for public display. I cannot make your husband acceptable before the eyes of Man. But before God, I swear to you, Phyllis, I assure you, Ralph will be like the driven snow."

How all the spectators cried, during the funeral, when he repeated that comment. Because of the rigor mortis, Ralph's coffin had to be squared like a packing box, into which he was pushed and jimmied till he fit. Then, because he could not be thrust through the usual narrow slot for the fiery furnace, cremation had to be done outside, in front of a hundred well-wishers, on a bonfire built from pine boughs within a perfect circle of rocks. His two best friends, the ones who tried to save him with six hours of CPR, they were the ones who constructed that stone circle as though it were their last campsite together. As the flames licked higher and higher, they all backed away from the searing heat and sang, en masse, "Old Flames Can't Hold A Candle To You."

It was a tearful, yet joyful, celebration of Ralph's finest hour, of the sacrifice he made for his buddies, on the last portage he ever made, as a canoeist, a dentist, a friend, a shield.

the earlier misfortunes of justin peach

"*PEACH*."

"That's a name that just oozes all the good things about life," said Aaron Stoodley. "Oozes it. Our Justin must be an aberration, for a Peach."

If he'd been born a Lemon, then that's what you'd expect, misery. That was Aaron's opinion, and Clyde Grandy's too. They looked up Lemon in the phonebook but there were none of them. Nobody wanted names like that. There were lots and lots of Peaches though, a half-column of them, sweet Peaches who they all figured lived in innocence. No Peaches waiting to fall from a tree, or rot on the ground, or get filled up with wasps and honeybees and then get flattened by the next boot that walked through the grass. Like for Apples. Peaches had to be optimists, they figured. For a test case, Aaron phoned up some of the anonymous Peaches and every one of those people sounded happy.

"We're taking a survey," Aaron said, "are you happy with your lot these days?"

"Oh yes," they said, "things could hardly be better for us."

So there it was. The Peaches were a jolly crew even though for some of them— most particularly for Justin Peach, the Peach we knew best—things didn't work out too well in the long run.

The very first time, no one could blame poor Justin. For one thing, he was only three years old. For another, his father never should have rented that little house out in the Battery. Didn't he look up that hill, up the cliff? That's what it was, really, a cliff, perpendicular, straight up and down with ridges too narrow for a goat. He signed the rent form on the dotted line but the cliff still loomed over the house like it was Mount Everest. The sun never shone there. Didn't Justin's father see the big rocks, some of them way bigger than the poor little house itself, hanging up there balanced on nothing, hanging like the raised Sword of Damocles? The house was affordable, sure, but it was made out of sticks, and there was no way it could have stood up to the force of what happened. Didn't he read the history books, the avalanches that swept down in winter storms? Well, I guess he didn't. Why should he? It had been there seventy-five years, they said afterwards, crossing themselves. The house lasted that long partly because there were so many holes between the boards that it offered up no resistance to the wind that blew threw it at a hundred miles an hour. Justin's father wasn't worried about that. He was in town at last. He had no concerns about the Hand of God, the Sword of Damocles, the Toss of the Dice, the Monkey's Paw, or any of the things that maybe he should have. He was just looking forward to the new job he had up there at the Battery Motel, where he was the new handyman.

"This job looks good," he said the first night he came home and the eight of them opened the door for him to see how it went.

"There's work there for two hundred years," he said, "break out the rum."

They threw some more wood in the stove and the snow started outside with the fading of the light. The storm broke all records by midnight and, in the morning, at breakfast, it was still a white-out outside the window.

"Put Justin in the chair over there," his father said to the uncles and the aunts and to his wife and to the two older girls.

Those were the last words he spoke, or any of those uncles, aunts, or girls spoke, or Mrs. Peach spoke, lifetime. The rumble lasted one second, that's all, long enough for them to turn their heads before one of those big rocks and the snow that feathered all around it sheared through the house and took it all—except for the part Justin was in—lock, stock, and barrel into the slob ice that blew up against the edge of the harbour. Down through that ice too, so all there was a half hour later was a piece of the roof floating cock-eyed out by Chain Rock. In the grip of the tide it was, heading outwards. Nobody ever saw any of them again, not even their mortal bodies, and only Justin was still there in his chair when the neighbours came in their undershirts, hurrying and looking up the hill with their eyes all wild. "Justin was crying a bit," they said, "and cold, but right away he smiled." He smiled his way into their hearts, at least for a while. He was adopted by the nearest ones, name of Poole, but they left him with the name Peach because it was his, and he was the last one of that particular bunch.

"You're some peach," they always said to him when things were good.

On the other hand, when things weren't so good, even when he did nothing wrong, his stepmother, Alice Poole, would look at him with her eyes flashing and she'd say, "Poison, Poison, that's the name you should have been born with. Oh what in Christ has brought me this boy." No, she was not a warm, a supportive woman.

When he was older, Justin would walk out onto his new porch and look at the gap next door where the rock ran through.

"How'd you like to experience something like that?" asked Aaron Stoodley. "You know that image of a fish out of water, gasping on rocks? I bet it was like that, for him."

"I can see that," said Clyde Grandy.

The second big thing that went wrong for Justin Peach came on a lot slower than the avalanche but an argument could be made, according to Aaron, that this problem was even worse. It struck into the heart of his growing, his cringing years, when there was nothing he could do. He must have felt it all happening, totally unlike that fall of rock and snow which was fast, clean and painless really, not the slow throttling that now went on day in and day out in that new house of his in the Battery. Ten years of it went by and then Alice Poole couldn't take it anymore. "Poison," was all she said. She destroyed all the books in the house. She destroyed crayons and drawings and homework and the posters Justin had up in the bedroom, posters of hockey players, Metallica. She emptied all the wooden toys they owned— the older children were all gone now—she emptied them out one morning over the edge of the porch, where they slid and bounced into the harbour in an eerie replay of the first disaster that orphaned Justin Peach. He wasn't there to see it, thank God for him, but he was there when he came home from grade seven and there was the lady from the Children's Aid with her little car, and the professional way she had, brisk really, who explained to Justin that it was time to move on.

"But I was adopted," Justin said to her. "I was adopted. This is my family."

"Well, not really," she said, "you were only fostered here. That's why you're a Peach and not a Poole. Now it's time for somewhere else."

She moved him in with a family out Topsail Road, so now for

the first time there was no harbour to look at, no gap in the row of houses that clung to the side of the hill. There were just cars and houses and patchwork lawns and a new school and still, the report from the Children's Aid said, still Justin smiled with the new family and was right at home, right away. Perfect. There was no need for regular official check-ups out Topsail Road. That boy was as resilient as Indian rubber.

Yes, Justin Peach fit in real well. All the kids were fostered there, in that particular house on Topsail Road. There was no nuclear family. It was wild and warm and carefree and normal for them all, that kind of life. There were twelve of them, and the washer and the dryer went non-stop. At least forty pieces of toast had to be margarined every morning by those children who'd come from everywhere, and there in that kitchen they used a wide paint brush, according to Aaron Stoodley who once wandered into it himself by mistake, and everybody took their turn. Toast-maker. One by one, they'd dip that wide paint brush into the melted so-called butter that simmered there in a pot on the front burner, and then they slapped the drippings over all the toast they wanted. Peanut butter, jam, fruit spread, everything within reason. There was nothing wrong with that. It was good. The trouble was, after he was there just two weeks, Justin went out one evening with the oldest boy there, Michael, who said he'd show him the neighbourhood.

"Let's look around," Michael said.

They walked down Patrick Street and Michael said, "Look, down there is where the harbour's at," and Justin Peach tried to see the old Battery and the Poole house through a gap in the houses, but he couldn't. He was too short.

While Justin Peach was doing that, his new friend Michael casually reached down to the curbside and picked up a piece of broken stone the size of a duck's egg. He threw that rock real hard through the nearest front window of a fancy house, painted yellow, just three feet away. Justin Peach heard the noise and said, "What's that?" but Michael was running off down the hill and turned the corner, out of sight. That boy could run. It was like he was never there, he vanished so fast. Justin just sat down on the curb because he didn't know what to do. He never saw the Battery that day, that's for sure. A man came out of the house with the selfsame rock in his hand and then a police car came up the road and the policeman took Justin Peach by the neck of the coat and said, "What's with that, you little fucker?"

He took the boy right off down to the station and that's how Justin Peach, though totally innocent of any wrongdoing, got into the justice system for the first time. Actually, it was the only time, Aaron Stoodley said, as far as he knew, and really Justin Peach was just by-catch in the wide-thrown nets of the constabulary. He wasn't the main target. If Justin Peach had told the truth, he'd have had no juvenile record at all. He didn't talk much though at the best of times, and when things got bad, Justin Peach could barely talk at all. He ended up taking the hit for that new friend of his. That's the way it was on Topsail Road, the unspoken code. He lived there for four more years, on probation, and everybody in the neighbourhood knew he was on the wrong side of the law. He got some tattoos, some facial piercings, a tongue stud, and he wore his hair in some pretty weird ways, with gel and various colours of dye. A Mohawk. Of course he went back to the yellow house on Patrick Street on a regular basis, on the order of the court, and there he paid off the window he never broke with some yard work out back.

"Funny," the owners said, "he doesn't seem the type of boy to just up and smash things. If anything, he's gentle."

The owners got along fine with Justin Peach after the initial episode with the stone. When Justin left the foster house on Topsail Road, when he turned sixteen and was cast out into the world, the owners of the yellow house said, "Hey Justin, you want the basement apartment?"

"Sure," he said, and he and a friend of his, Philip John Savoury, both of them now in welding school, moved right into the same house that had turned Justin Peach into the little criminal that a lot of ignorant people thought he was.

"That can happen to anyone," said Aaron. "People get the wrong impression. You're always the same to those who cannot see."

The fourth bad thing that happened to Justin Peach, and the worst of them all, arguably, up until then (forget the much-later pizza party and the botulism and the death of the whole soccer team in Halifax) was how he lost his first real girlfriend, Rhynie Lights. She was a lively girl he met at high school and she had a family that lived up above Military Road. It was a real nice family. After a while, though she was nervous about it, she invited Justin to come along to this and that, to a picnic, to a party, and all of Rhynie's family were there. They accepted him, more or less, and then one day they invited him to Thanksgiving dinner. He'd never been anywhere like that, what with the turkey and maybe twelve of them all told sitting round the table, saying grace, cranberry sauce, gravy, potatoes and peas, the big difference being they were all related to each other, not like the hodge-podge on Topsail Road, where nearly always somebody would flip out half-way through the meal to the merriment of some. There, at Rhynie's, no one seemed out of sorts, no one said, "Well fuck you too," and started crying and throwing mashed potatoes and running upstairs while the foster parents said, "There, there, settle down, boys will be boys." Rhynie's home was like a dream by comparison. Mind you, Justin Peach was grateful for those mostly-pleasant times on Topsail Road, but they were, when he looked back upon them, wild and even savage compared to the nice glassware, the laughs, Rhynie's father tossing back a few, the easy times that a real family seemed to have, without even trying.

After Thanksgiving dinner was over and the dishes were all washed and dried by Rhynie and her mother, Justin and Rhynie went out together and walked around the corner to where he'd left his third-hand motorcycle parked by the curb. They never left it anywhere near Rhynie's house. Rhynie's mother hated bikers and everything they stood for. It was one of her pet peeves. She couldn't separate, in her mind, the difference between a biker and a boy with a motorcycle, but Rhynie herself, to Justin's great good fortune, had instinctively known the difference. So, that Thanksgiving night, when he said, "Jump on, Rhynie, one spin downtown and I'll bring you right back," she said, "Okay," and jumped on, both of them without helmets because the helmets were back on Patrick Street, hanging from the coatrack. "Go slow," she said, and he did go slow but that was a particular night that going slow wasn't good enough, because the temperature had dropped to freezing and there was, down at the corner of Military Road and Bonaventure, a broken water hydrant that sent a spray of water, invisible to all that went by, fanning out across the curve where the road dipped into the turn, and the water landed on the asphalt and froze there in a band maybe four feet wide, like a river across the intersection. No one could see it, the frozen river of black ice, and all the cars that went by drove over it without a problem. It was as black as the night itself and there were leaves blowing across it like a rustling shroud when Justin's motorcycle banked into the turn. The wheels had nothing to grip on and down they went. Rhynie was thrown off to the right and her head hit the curb with what must have been an awful sound, had anybody been there to hear it, and Justin was knocked out too, his head skinned along the pavement.

"Maybe it was the gel in his Mohawk that saved him," Aaron said, "because of the reduced friction. He slid rather than banged."

All the news wasn't bad though, despite the obvious horror of the accident, because when the police and the ambulance came and the policeman said, "This girl doesn't look good, put on the siren boys," a car pulled over and a man got out and walked over and bent down and looked at Rhynie. He had a little flashlight with him and he opened the upper lids of her eyes and flashed the light in.

"This girl's going to die," he said, "there's only one thing to do."

He ran back to his car and he came back with a Canadian Tire bag and he spilled it all out on the pavement and from that he got out one of those hand-held power drills.

"I just bought this," he said, "by a miracle, ten minutes ago. These drills are clean as a whistle."

"Wait a minute," said the policeman.

"Officer, I'm a neurosurgeon," the man said, "and this girl's going to die. Back off."

He pulled on the trigger of the drill and it revved up and he carefully put his thumb on the side of Rhynie's head. He felt around and then full speed with the drill, drilled it through her dark hair, through her skull, just over top of her left ear. Skull-bits curled out over the tiny fake-pearl earring that she always wore there, and chewed bone and blood came out of that drill-hole in a long ooze. The neurosurgeon looked at her eyes again with the little light.

"Now take her to the hospital, I'll be there," the man said.

Red lights flashed around them in the darkness.

"Take the boy too, he'll be all right."

One operation later, Rhynie was okay. She recovered perfectly in every way except for the fact that she lost her memory for the night of the accident, and for everything that happened to her in the six months previously. That included her whole relationship with Justin Peach. He might as well never have existed. When she woke up from the coma, her family said, "You're off to Toronto, to recuperate." Off she went. She never saw or gave a thought to Justin Peach again. For her, he never existed.

"And that was," said Aaron Stoodley, "a recurrent theme in the life of Justin Peach, like a minor chord that lingered in the air."

The policeman filled out a charge for careless driving that night, right on the spot, against Justin Peach, but then another officer, also on a motorcycle, pulled up and hit the same black ice and he spun out and fell too. He had a helmet on, and only broke his arm. So they tore the ticket up and you might say Justin got off easy that time.

"Got off easy?" said Aaron. "You'd only say that if you didn't know how Justin felt about Rhynie."

Because Rhynie was by far the best thing that had ever happened to him. When she went to Toronto, he lay there for a week in bed on Patrick Street, in the basement. He couldn't smile anymore. He felt as though something had torn through him, like the avalanche that just missed him when he was a baby, like the rock and the snow that ripped through his family's house, through the house that was so skimpy, so threadbare, so poor that it never should have been built on the face of this earth at all.

breathing like that

I AM WRITING late at night when it's easy: no one remembers it but us, even the gibbous moon which in that rare sky blew down the path—and lit it up the way we felt—forgot it, as did the owl who turned away, small and dark over the wind-ripped black water of Soldier's Pond, so high above the city, so high we were, the line of surf laced all the way to Cappahayden, and the grass laid out horizontal by our breathing like that.

acknow-
ledgements

Thanks, with love, to Cheryl, for bringing these stories together, to Nora and Jess for their acumen and support, to Willy and James.

Thanks, also with love, to Tom and Martha Keeping for taking care of me when I lived in Belleoram, to their children Tommy and Estella, to William May Sr., Sarah May, William Jr.

Thanks to James Langer, editor, and to everyone at Breakwater: Rebecca Rose, Elisabeth de Mariaffi, Rhonda Molloy.

Thanks to Martha Webb, of Anne McDermid Agency, in Toronto.

Thank you: *The Antigonish Review*, *The Fiddlehead*, *The Dalhousie Review*, *subTerrain*, *Event*, *Prism International*, and the *Journey Prize Anthology*, in which some of these stories first appeared.

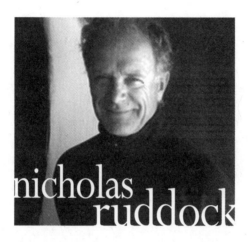

Nicholas Ruddock's award-winning poetry and fiction have been widely published in Canada and abroad. His story "How Eunice Got Her Baby" appeared in the Journey Anthology 19 and was produced by the Canadian Film Centre. His novel, *The Parabolist* (Doubleday, 2010), was shortlisted for the Toronto Book Award. Ruddock lives in Guelph, Ontario.